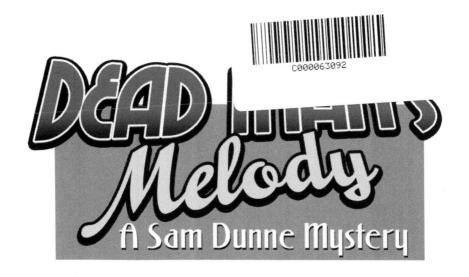

DEAD MAN'S Melody
A Sam Dunne Mystery

C000063092

AIRSHIP 27 PRODUCTIONS

Dead Man's Melody
© 2016 Fred Adams Jr.

Published by Airship 27 Productions
www.airship27.com
www.airship27hangar.com

Interior illustrations © 2016 Richard Jun
Cover illustration © 2016 Rob Davis

Editor: Ron Fortier
Associate Editor: Gordon Dymowski
Marketing and Promotions Manager: Michael Vance
Production and design by Rob Davis.

ISBN-10: 0-9977868-5-X
ISBN-13: 978-0-9977868-5-9

Printed in the United States of America

10 9 8 7 6 5 4 3 2 1

Fred Adams Jr.

The best laid plans fall subject to ambition
Trial and error, the layman's attrition
Is today's remedy
A dead man's melody no radio will play?

- Eric Corday, "Life in Double Time"

Let me make a suggestion.

Ask yourself this question: Do you really think you could kill someone?

If you have never been to the edge, you can't know the answer, even though you may think you do. If you have been there, then you already know.

That is a touchy question. It plumbs self-image issues most of us would rather leave alone, disturbs the sediment of a complacent pool. The answer may make you proud, ashamed, or afraid.

The question is touchier still when the person who asks it is a homicide detective.

Let me tell you a story . . .

1

I was almost through my arm and chest routine at The Pump House, the barbell club where I lift, when the call came. I just finished three sets of inclined presses and the sweat circles on my ratty Ramones T-shirt were about to merge into one dark mass. I keep the volume high on the ringer because after thirty-odd years of playing in rock bands, my ears are a little bit dull. But the obnoxious ring tone, a clip from Funkadelic's "Maggot Brain" always manages to cut through the clank and clatter.

When my cell phone rings with a number I don't know, it's rarely good news. I should probably leave the damned thing shut off, but I keep it on anyway as a nod to the inevitable. When I answer it, I feel as if I'm sticking my hand in a hollow log and wondering what may bite me. That morning the call was no exception.

"Yeah."

"Sam?"

"You got me. Who's this?"

"Cotton."

I knew Bill "Cotton" Breakiron from working with him in a half dozen bands over the past twenty years. He played a mean tenor sax and gravitated between old style rhythm and blues and jazz.

"You didn't show up on my caller I.D. Thought you were the Phantom."

"New phone. Listen, Sam, did you hear the news? Eddie Shay's dead. Somebody shot him."

I didn't know quite how to take that. Eddie Shay, my former band mate from Gin Sing left me behind fifteen years ago when he and Danny Barton booted me aside on their way to a sort of mid-range stardom.

"When did this happen, Cotton?"

"Last night. The cops are calling it murder. Story is they found some coke around the body. They're saying maybe a 'dealer's disagreement.'"

I walked out of the weight room into the foyer away from the noise. I was around Eddie for a long time, and except for the occasional recreational joint, he wasn't much for drugs, but people change. "That doesn't sound like Eddie to me. He was more the bourbon type."

"I hear you. But the cops find one line of flake, and it's case closed, you know?"

"Damn. That's bizarre. But, if it wasn't drugs, who'd want to kill Eddie, except for a dozen or so jilted women or angry husbands?" Heads turned on the two guys signing in and the girl behind the desk, and I realized I'd better keep my voice down. Sometimes when your hearing's going, you don't realize how loud you talk.

"I couldn't guess, Sam. You knew him better than I did."

"I haven't seen him much lately. You did some session work for him and Danny last year didn't you?"

"Yeah, but I didn't spend much quality time with them." Cotton segued into his lawn jockey affect. "They don't *con*sort much wit' de hired help. Felt like I's back on de *plan*tation."

"You and everybody else; you don't work with those two, you work for them. Thanks for the word, Cotton. "

"Always better to hear bad news from a friend than from the radio."

"Yeah. You still at the Regent?"

"Friday through Sunday; come check it out."

"Will do. Don't let your lip slip."

"Cold day in hell, dude."

I snapped the phone shut. Beth, the little brunette working the desk looked up from her Sandra Brown paperback. "Bad news, Sam?"

"No, just news." Time for an existential decision: do I reverently suspend my Saturday workout, go home and put on a black armband? I headed for the dumbbell rack instead.

Eddie was dead. Murdered? I was surprised but not shocked. When you work around creative people, performers, artists, you learn a lot about egos. Most of us have big egos, but there are two types. The first, Eddie's type, was so big that it didn't leave room for anyone else. The second type, the kind I'd like to think I have, is even bigger; so big that it wraps around everybody and you're all welcome, but sometimes egos clash and bad things happen.

I looked around the weight room. I guess barbell clubs are temples to the ego, too. If not, why all the mirrors? You have the young muscle heads who think they have to shock and awe. Then there are the really strong, ripped guys who don't have to look at themselves to know what they have: grace with no need of motion; power with no need of effort; excellence with no need of recognition. In the end, the only person you have to impress is yourself, whether you're pumping iron, playing guitar or painting houses. Too bad most people never learn that.

Tom Denzel traded off with me on the inclined bench doing dumbbell flys. Tom and I grew up together. He's in his late forties like me, and both of us are fighting thinning hair, gravity and Taco Bell. His T-shirt was as sweat-soaked as mine. "You think we're getting too old for this shit, Dunne?" He grinned. Unlike me, he was missing a few teeth.

"Like the gun nut bumper stickers say, Tom, 'from my cold dead hand.' You and I'll have pulley weights on our wheelchairs in the old age home."

"If somebody doesn't shoot us first," he quipped. I guess he hadn't heard the news.

I laughed, but not too much. The joke hit a nerve. I finished my set and headed for the showers.

2

There are days when I think I might want a house then I remind myself that I don't need a mortgage, taxes and a lawn to mow. My apartment is on the third floor of a four-story building. The neighbors on my floor are yuppies who go to some office every day, which works out well for me. It's quiet into the afternoon so that I can write and record, and my noise doesn't bother any late sleepers. About the time they're walking in with a computer bag over one shoulder, I'm walking out with a guitar under my arm headed for a gig, a convenient arrangement.

I put on a pot of coffee and flipped through my mail. I feel the same way about mail as I do about answering my phone. No major stuff: my cell phone bill, a catalog, two credit card offers and a reminder from my dentist that it was time to get my teeth cleaned. I poured a cup of coffee and did something I rarely do. I put the old Gin Sing demo cassette in the deck. I keep telling myself that I should copy it onto a CD, if only to protect the recording, but somehow it seems sacrilegious.

There I was. There we were: Eddie and Danny's harmonies and my lead guitar. I walked back to the kitchen and pulled the bottle of Yukon Jack out of the cabinet over the stove and poured a slug into my coffee. "Cold Fire" came on with my signature riff and Eddie's husky tenor jumped in over it. "Your love is a cold fire. Burn me out while you chill my soul." Maybe not my best song ever, but it was good enough to make the LP when Eddie and Danny signed with Sunsong Records and stepped over me on their way out the door to fame.

I raised my cup in a toast. "So long, Eddie. Can't say it was great, but it did happen."

My living room testifies to my divided self. The furniture is eclectic, a diplomatic word for yard sale chic. Wives get the furniture, husbands get the bills. People offer me a couch, an end table, a lamp that's outlived their taste, and it's usually better than the one I have, certainly too good to throw away, and I'm living a second-hand life. But the old blue sofa bed, the nicked up coffee table and the scuffed leather lounger aren't my focus in the room.

One wall is hung with a dozen instruments, guitars, basses, mandolins, a banjo and even a ukulele. Another is lined with bookcases full of the great works of English Literature. I'm a musician first, but it never hurts to have a backup.

I remember trombonist Steve Turre telling a group of high schoolers at a jazz clinic to get an education and a marketable skill before they try to tackle the pro music scene, especially in New York or L.A. If not, in his words, "in six months you'll be dead or selling drugs." He's right. I got my English degree in the eighties and went on for a Master's so that I could teach college courses. When the music business is slow, I teach an occasional bonehead composition class at Hanniston Area Community College (known locally by its unfortunate acronym) to pay bills. Lately, I've also picked up extra cash bootlegging term papers for an online essay mill.

Making a piecemeal living at a lot of different things demands a form of self-discipline that most people lack. That's why an old joke defines the difference between an amateur musician and a professional one: the amateur musician has a full-time day job; the professional musician has a wife with a full-time day job. Somehow I get away with neither one.

I sipped my coffee and sat with a pocket notebook and a pencil jotting down things that I needed to do. I hate to admit it, but at forty-eight, I have to write things down before they get away. The demo ended, the silence was oppressive, and my coffee tasted bitter. What to do on a Thursday afternoon? I decided to take a walk down the street and do something else I rarely do, buy a newspaper. I pulled a sweater over my T-shirt and slipped on my shoes.

There's a difference between looking at yourself in the wall of mirrors in a gym and the little eighteen-by-twelve over the bathroom sink. I never see guys walk up to the big mirrors for a close look at their noses or teeth, but they'll put their faces two inches from the small ones. Every time I look in one, I look older, so I try to ignore them, but today Eddie's death reminded me of my own mortality. I stopped for a minute by the door and took a hard look at Sam Dunne.

More grey, more crow's feet, more nose hair, grizzlier eyebrows. If I shaved my beard, I'd look ten years younger. If I dyed my hair, I'd look ten years younger. If I took Botox injections, I'd look ten years younger but for what? My looks didn't get me very far when I was young. How far will they get me now that I'm old? At least that's one thing Eddie won't have to worry about anymore, kinda like Sam Cooke.

The hallway was as silent as my apartment, so much so that the ding of the elevator startled me. I stepped into the car and saw a hazy version of me in the polished steel of the walls. Some well-intentioned soul stuffed a Bible tract in a gap between the panels. The title boldly proclaimed in flaming red letters, "God Doesn't Want You to Go to Hell!" Well, that makes two of us.

Out on the street, the world looked as little like Hell as it could in Hanniston, Pennsylvania. "The sun is out. The sky is blue. It's beautiful, and so are you," I thought as a twenty-something in black and yellow spandex rollerbladed past me on the sidewalk, swaying in time to whatever private rhythms pulsed in her ear buds. Her boyfriend zipped past me a few seconds later. Their outfits matched, but their movements didn't. Her body twisted gracefully. She was listening to something sinuous and syncopate. His legs pumped like pistons, force personified. He was listening to something aggressive and linear. Beyonce and Metallica? Norah Jones and

Lynard Skynyrd? They were sharing the day without sharing themselves; a metaphor for our times.

T. S. Eliot wrote that April is "the cruelest month." The IRS aside, I disagree. October seems worse to me. Indian Summer speaks of last chances before the cold sets in, of the need to hurry because any day the snow will fall. Life as a set of seasons is a cliché, but most clichés are clichés because they ring true enough to be repeated. The warm sun on my face was a tease. It showed me not what was coming, but what was going away.

I walked a few blocks to the Mini Mart and looked over the newspapers on the rack. Eddie's death obviously didn't make the front page of the *New York Times*, but the locals both carried Eddie's death—call it what it was – Eddie's murder—on page one. I grabbed a copy of the *Herald* and the *Sentinel* and headed for the counter where the clerk was arguing with a young girl in a green windbreaker and a knit cap about selling cigarettes to her without an I.D.

"Look man," she said, "I'm twenty-two. I lost my driver's license and didn't get the replacement from the DMV yet."

The clerk, a guy about my age, who looked positively emasculated by the red Mini Mart vest, pointed to a sign: If you look under 30, you must have a valid I.D. to purchase tobacco products. "You see the sign. That's our policy." He turned to me, dismissing the girl and pointed to the papers. "Anything else?"

"Yeah," I said. I turned to the kid. "What brand do you want?"

"Marlboros."

I turned back to the clerk. "The papers and a pack of Marlboros. Want to card me too?"

He opened his mouth to say something then thought better of it and turned to the cigarette shelves. He glared at me and rang up the purchase. I handed her the cigarettes and held out my hand for her money. I paid the clerk, and she and I walked out together. "Thanks, man."

"No problem. You probably shouldn't smoke anyway, but it just pisses me off when people use the word 'policy' to dodge dealing with life."

She nodded, smiling. "I hear you. Thanks again. Have a good one."

As she walked away, I wondered, a good *what*?"

3

The papers were full of it. The *Sentinel's* headline spanned the top of the page: **LOCAL ROCKER MURDERED**. Below, two articles dominated the page, one about the murder itself, and the other a retrospective piece about Eddie's music and Gin Sing. The crime story was short and concise. Not much known yet, investigation continuing, no suspects, possibly drug related. You can't blame the reporters; the cops will, by default, sit on the info for a while in the hope that they'll catch a break if the bad guys don't know how much they know. The retrospective on Eddie was an elaborate obituary that painted him as a minor deity. The phrase "rock star" appeared three or four times in the piece, and words like "composer," "songwriter," and "virtuoso" popped up from time to time. They left out "asshole."

I really shouldn't be so hard on Eddie. You could no more blame him for things he did than you could a dog that chews your slippers. It was just his nature. Eddie could never be anything but what he was, as plenty of women learned the hard way over the years. He broke hearts as a hobby, trading on his looks and his rock idol status.

The article included a comment from "band mate and collaborator" Danny Barton: "God, it's horrible. I'm still in shock. I hope they fry whoever did this." I was miffed. Nobody asked me what I thought; maybe they were afraid of what I might say about the hometown superstar.

I could tell them about three a.m. fifteen years ago in the back of the band truck, Eddie on his hands and knees heaving with sobs and vomit, crying because he was drunk and sick with fear. It took me a long time after to understand that what he feared was succeeding and people seeing him as he saw himself, a fake, an unworthy impostor. That's why he never let any woman get too close, for fear she'd see through him and blow the whistle. He hid his anxiety behind a façade of large-living bravado and kept it bay with the bottle.

The picture that ran with the piece as it continued on page two showed Eddie in his prime; bare-chested and sweating, hair flying, mouth open in a snarl as his right hand raked the strings of his Les Paul. Every inch the bad boy, and it was all a calculated performance.

The *Herald* carried the headline story on the front page and featured a full page on the front of section two with photos and a bio. They were less laudatory, but not by much. The *Herald* ran a bunch of carefully selected man-on-the-street quotes from admiring fans, most of them variations on the "Eddie was great" theme. No surprises there. But they did run an old Gin Sing photo at the bottom of the page. Eddie stood in the middle, and I slouched at the left end, a study in surly, long-haired insouciance. Under the picture, the cut line misspelled my last name.

The evening news was full of it too. Gin Sing was probably the biggest thing to ever come from Hanniston, and Eddie Shay was the better part of Gin Sing. The reporter stood on Eddie's front lawn solemnly intoning the story as lights strobed in the background from police cars and an ambulance. "And here, local rock musician Eddie Shay was brutally murdered... Police sources say that drugs may be involved . . . at this hour little is known but the investigation continues . . ."

Back in the studio the pretty boy anchor said, "Fellow Gin Sing member Danny Barton was unavailable for comment." The station then ran thirty seconds of an old MTV clip of Gin Sing playing live right after their first LP was released. Eddie, tall, lean and handsome, belted out "Fool for Myself" while behind him, Danny Barton windmilled his guitar. The song ended to thunderous applause, and Pretty Boy looked somberly into the camera. "A happier time for Eddie Shay, dead at thirty-nine."

I switched off the TV and stared at the blank screen.

My cell phone rang and I decided to let it go to voice mail. I didn't feel much like talking, and the caller I.D. showed the word "Restricted." Three rings and the phone quit before voicemail kicked in. The same thing happened every fifteen minutes for the next two hours. I thought maybe I should get an unlisted number and I decided that maybe what I needed was an unlisted life.

4

It was a given that I'd get yanked in as at least a secondary suspect. My past with Eddie Shay was less than friendly, particularly since the band took off soon after they dumped me. They got rich and famous and I stayed a working man. A detective named Mike Kearny called me three days after the murder and asked me to come to the station. The fact that they called in old news like me told me the cops didn't have much.

The precinct station looks like a movie set for a dentist's office. The City spent a of couple million taxpayer bucks to dress up its public buildings. The result was just pimped up institutional chic. New carpet, new paint, new furniture, old ceiling tile—like changing into a tux and leaving your athletic socks on your feet.

Kearny came out after the requisite twenty minute wait. Show me who's in charge. He looked close to my age; tall, gangly, maybe played second-string basketball in high school. He wore standard cop couture: tan JC Penney's suit, those sensible black shoes that cops learn to love walking a beat, and a badly tied striped tie. At least it wasn't a clip-on. His lean face was clean shaven and his sandy hair was short and unruly.

Kearny gave a point away when he waved me back without confirming my name. He knew me by sight already; either that or because I was the only person in the lobby without handcuffs on my belt or my wrists. The sergeant buzzed me through the security gate, and I followed Kearny into a small windowless room with a number three on the door, a table and a few chairs. No ashtray. I hate smoking bans though I haven't smoked a cigarette for twenty years.

"So, Mr. Dunne—may I call you Sam?" Kearny said in an adenoidal voice.

I didn't respond and he took it for tacit approval. He didn't offer me coffee, which meant he already got my prints from one place or another and didn't have to trick me into giving them to him on a china mug. There was no two-way glass or mirror in the room, but I figured Kearny's buddies were watching me on candid camera.

"We thought maybe you could help us out with your friend's case." No response. "Eddie was your friend, right?"

"'Was' is correct," I said in a flat voice, "in more ways than one. He quit being my friend years ago, and then he just quit being, or somebody quit it for him."

Kearny gave me a tight-lipped, mirthless smile. "Did that bother you?"

"'Bad news on the doorstep, I couldn't take one more step.' Hell, no. One day we're born, one day we die. I have no feelings one way or the other. He's gone. I'm not."

"That's pretty cold. Maybe you oughta feel some satisfaction. After all, he and Danny Barton kicked you out of the band. You know, I used to hang out at Rocco's in the old days when you still played for Gin Sing. They were good. You were good. Why'd they dump you?"

"You'll laugh. The record guys came around in the age of the Hair Band; they wanted young. I was out already of grad school when I teamed up with them. By the time the record deal came, I was in my thirties—old man in the band; bad for the image. Get rid of me or no contract. They thought it over for about thirty seconds and pulled my plug. Guess that didn't make the *Rolling Stone* story."

Kearny nodded and pulled a can of Skoal out of his pocket. He put a pinch in his cheek and I wondered where he was going to spit in that empty room. "Must've made you angry."

"I'm a big boy. I got past it."

"Yeah, but they made big bucks. What do you make?"

I stared him down. "An honest living."

And so Kearny and I danced for an hour as he plied the standard cop-interrogation technique: poke and provoke. Poke until you find a sore spot and then gouge at it until the perp boils over with fear, rage, frustration, whatever. Like most cops he told little and asked everything. Where was I on the night of the murder? Could I provide proof? When was the last time I saw Eddie? Did Eddie have any enemies? Did I own a dog? Finally Kearny came down to it.

"You carry, Sam?"

I shrugged. "I have a permit."

He reran his tight-lipped grin. "That's not what I asked. Do you carry?"

"Sometimes."

"Why?"

I shrugged again and put my palms on the table. "Places I work, you boys show up about the time trouble's over and the bad guys are lying on the floor. I'm there when it starts and I'm sitting in a goddammed spotlight."

".25 Beretta automatic, right?" I didn't respond. I knew he knew. My permit and pistol registry were on file. Kearny looked to be the type to do his homework. He pushed his lower lip under his upper one and nodded, looking down at the table. "That about does it," he said, smiling. Then his head tipped up and he smiled more broadly, this time showing teeth. "For now."

I was almost out the door when he said, "Sam." I turned and we locked eyes. "Do you really think you could kill someone?" It was bait, one alpha male taunting another, a last try to piss me off and make me say the wrong thing.

I did a silent three-count and gave him a hard stare. "Don't know. Never been there."

He did a three-count of his own, nodded and said, "Right."

I couldn't tell for sure whether Kearny knew I was lying.

By the way, the jerk spat on the new floor tile.

• • •

Years ago when I was younger and wilder, I used to score weed from a dealer on Prospect Avenue. I never knew his name, but I called him "Jones" for my own frame of reference. You rolled down Prospect, slowed at the 12th Street intersection, and blinked your turn signals left-right-left-right. If he knew your car, Jones would dart out of the shadows like a ferret, reach in your window with a bag of grass in one hand and take your cash with the other. Five seconds, and you both were gone.

One night, someone decided to start a new enterprise. I pulled up in my old Chevy Nova and signaled, but instead of Jones, a guy in a hoodie ran out, reached in my window, and put a screwdriver at my throat. "Give me your wallet, motherfucker."

I was a little stronger and a little quicker than he expected. I grabbed his weapon hand and pulled him half into the window then I floored it. I got the car up to about 35 or 40 on Prospect, dragging him as I went. He screamed in my ear like a girl and kept it up until I wiped him off on the back corner of a big Ford LTD parked at the curb.

The cops found him a few hours later lying in the street looking like someone dumped a bag of laundry. I was lucky. He was a junkie named Thomas "Poogie" Washington with a long sheet full of crime and time. Instead of saying, "This demands further investigation," the cops decided that some anonymous citizen performed a public service and instead said, "Amen."

Once in a while I dream about that sound of him hitting the LTD, like a rotten tree falling in the woods. I wake up, remind myself he shoved a screwdriver under my chin, and roll over and go back to sleep.

Amen.

5

My cell phone woke me the next morning. For some reason I never remember to put it on the nightstand, and I have to play hide-and-seek with it every time it yanks me out of sleep like a hooked trout. "Yeah?"

"Sam Dunne?" A woman's voice, but not one I recognized.

"Yeah." Early morning conversation was not my long suit.

"This is Wendy Conn from the *Sentinel*."

"Yeah? What?" I was waking up and unpacking my repertoire.

"I hear Kearny called you in on the Shay murder. Comment?"

Rejecting "screw you," "up yours," and "buzz off," I opted for, "How'd you hear about that so fast?"

"Good sources," she said, in an unaffected, smoky voice. "So how about it? Got anything to say?"

"Who did you say you are?"

"Catherine Zeta-Jones—I said I'm Wendy Conn from the *Sentinel*."

That jolted me to full consciousness. I knew Wendy Conn as a local legend, though I'd never met her, a hard-assed reporter for the *Daily Sentinel* who covered the police beat with zeal and enthusiasm for stirring the cesspool that was local organized crime. When one of her exposes blew the lid off a local money laundering operation, she was brassy enough to stand on the sidewalk outside the station when the cops perp-walked Joey "Spuds" Sputelli. Sputelli yelled at her, "You're in a pile of trouble, bitch!" She sneered back at him, "I'll worry in twenty years, asshole." Her name was the byline on the *Sentinel's* story about Eddie's murder. I told her I had nothing to say.

"Then why did Kearny pull you in?"

"He was doing what cops always do when they have zip—fishing. Did you ask him why?"

"He's next. I wanted to give you a chance first before he tars your stellar reputation with innuendo."

"It's too early in the day for words like 'innuendo.'" I yawned broad and loud.

"How about lunch? Does that give your brain time to engage? I'll buy."

"How friggin' generous."

"Not at all. I have an expense account. Dora's at twelve-thirty?"

"Okay, you win. Twelve-thirty at Dora's. Wear your press pass so I don't mistake you for a civilian." The phone clicked in my ear. I wondered whether she would invite Kearny along too. One way to find out.

• • •

Dora's is a restaurant that serves old style diner food 24-7. It's a family business, around since the fifties, serving hot roast beef sandwiches with mashed potatoes and gravy or bacon and eggs day or night. A long counter with old-fashioned pedestal stools shares a wide aisle with a dozen booths. Diners in the booths can look out the windows and watch the traffic on 15th Street. The stoolies can watch each other in the mirrors and harass the waitresses. I'd seen Wendy Conn's picture in the paper a few times, and I spotted her as soon as I walked in. She was in a back booth, face half-hidden behind an open laptop, sitting where she could watch the door.

I waved at Jenny, the counter girl as I passed. "Don't you ever go home?"

She gave me a sad smile and wiped a strand of red hair from her forehead. "To what? I don't even have a cat anymore. At least here there are faces and voices." She tilted her head a little and lowered her eyelids, "Of course, if somebody was there for me to come home to—." Her smile turned playful.

"As soon as I retire, I'll be back for you darlin'," I flirted. "'Grow old along with me, the best is yet to be . . .'"

She laughed and hugged herself, saying, "Oooh, I get all shivery when a guy quotes Browning." She rolled her eyes.

I rolled my eyes back at her. "And I get all shivery when a woman recognizes Browning."

"You aren't the only one who reads poetry," she smirked.

The order-up bell ended our repartee. As she sashayed over to pick up a plate of hash and home fries, she said over her shoulder, "I'll bring your coffee."

I dropped into the booth opposite Wendy Conn and she kept typing. Jenny brought the coffee, and in a minute Wendy closed the laptop and set it on the seat beside her. She reached her hand over the table as if I'd just arrived, no apologies. "Hi, Sam—Wendy Conn." Her grip was hard, and her eyes unflinching. I decided that her tough-gal reputation was probably well deserved.

She was maybe thirty-five and maybe forty. Wendy was short, I'd guess five-two, and compact in an athletic way. She obviously worked out and took good care of herself. Her honey-blonde hair was pulled back. She wore a denim Levi jacket over a pullover sweater and jeans. Makeup would have clashed with her hard-ass persona, but I could see that tricked out for dinner and dancing she'd look damned good.

"So tell me about Eddie." No foreplay; she got right to it.

"What's to tell?" I shrugged out of my bomber jacket and laid it on the seat. "I hardly saw him for fifteen years since the – I can't call it a breakup – dismissal?"

Wendy nodded. "Good word. And after you left the band?"

"Gin Sing got some mainstream airplay for a while, toured with a few big names, put out an LP every year or so, but never quite got on top of it." I idly stirred my coffee with my spoon.

Wendy Conn…kept typing.

"Bad management and tax problems knocked them down early on, and they never quite got it back."

"But they're still celebrities, right?"

"Around here, yeah; they still do a lot of shows and open for some names, but in L.A. or New York, they're an asterisk in the record books. I hear the most money they ever made was on a commercial jingle for Busch Beer. But you know all of this, right?"

She yanked me back on track abruptly. "So you had no contact with Eddie Shay?"

"I'd see Eddie once in a while at a club or a concert. He'd give me a hug, introduce me to his latest squeeze, and say we'd have to get together soon. I knew better and so did he. I guess he was being diplomatic."

"No hard feelings?" She was pulling a steno pad and a ball-point pen out of her bag, all the time looking me right in the eye. I decided this one would give Kearny a run for his money any day.

"Nothing homicidal." I was being cute and immediately realized my mistake. Never breaking eye contact, she jotted it verbatim on the pad. I went on, choosing my words with a little more care. "I learned a long time ago not to take things personally; it's just business. He never gave me a reason to be angry once I left the band. He never bad-mouthed me, never snubbed me..."

"That was Danny Barton's job, right?" She was good. Poke and provoke. "If I were going to shoot anybody, it would be Danny, not Eddie," she said, a statement, not a question. "You think whoever killed Eddie might have a bull's-eye painted on Danny too?"

"He's another story for another day. You know, you sound like Kearny."

She shrugged "He's a good cop and he does his job well."

"He knew my pedigree, right down to my gun size."

She nodded, stirring her tea. "He would. By the way, the murder weapon was a .38."

"Good news. That lets me off the hook."

"Unless you borrowed somebody else's gun." I could feel her eyes weighing me, gauging my response to her calculated throwaway line. She was cagey.

I passed on the bait. "Kearny interviewed me by himself. Don't those guys usually come in pairs, like salt and pepper shakers?"

"Funny you'd put it that way," she laughed. "Devon Wilson, Kearny's partner is black. Word is he's on leave because of a burst appendix, but he'll be back soon."

"So he's the nice cop?"

She let that one go unanswered. "Let's save time. What did you and Kearny talk about?"

There was a basic difference between them. Kearny was linear, one question setting up the next. Wendy fired questions all over the place, like a destroyer dropping depth charges. "We talked about Eddie and why I'm not guilty." I shrugged. "Maybe you should talk with Kearny instead of me. He could give you a rounder picture." My coffee was empty and I held the cup up for Jenny to see it.

"But he's not here and you are." She smiled like a barracuda, and looking up she saw Jenny scurrying over. "Let's order."

We continued the conversation while she tore into a grilled chicken salad and I enjoyed my usual meat loaf special. "You know that crap will clog your arteries," she said around a mouthful of lettuce. "Way too much cholesterol." She held her fork in her left hand while she kept the pen in her right, scribbling on her pad.

"Hasn't killed me yet," I shot back with a grin.

"'Yet' being the operative word. So, since you left Gin Sing, what have you done career-wise?"

"Lots of one-nighters in local clubs, some resort work, taught guitar lessons for a few years, a few studio sessions, some commercial jingles."

"Lots of small money." Poke. "And you're always scrambling for it."

"It pays bills. Besides, I still get royalty checks for 'Cold Fire' and 'Downhill Drift.' Thank God for Classic Rock radio and iTunes."

"But most of Gin Sing's hits were co-written by Shay and Barton, right?"

"Just like Lennon and McCartney."

"And that makes you what? George Harrison?"

I laughed, almost choking on my coffee. "I wish. At least he got to stay in the band."

"How does that make you feel?"

My smile flatlined. "Dispossessed."

Wendy's questions continued to swirl, but as the talk continued, they closed in on what she really wanted to ask.

"So who do you think killed Eddie?"

A thought crystallized: Kearny was her "good source" and maybe she was his. I gave her a three count. "No idea." I stood up. "Tell Kearny I said hello." I wiped my mouth with a napkin. "Thanks for lunch."

As I walked out, I could feel her eyes boring into the back of my skull. She wasn't used to someone else ending an interview, or anything else for that matter. I knew this wasn't the last time I'd talk to her, or Kearny.

On the way out, Jenny turned and smiled at me over her shoulder, and I caught myself wondering what she might look like under that pink rayon uniform.

I decided to leave the van in Dora's parking lot and walk the few blocks to Malone's Music. I don't buy a lot of new gear like some people do. I think they're making a mistake. The first thing young kids do when their bands catch on and they start making money is score that guitar they've always wanted or a bigger amp or PA system. Or they buy some effect pedal that makes them sound like Yngwe Malmsteen or Joe Satriani, whoever the current guitar hero may be. They're foolish; change your gear and you change the sound that got you work in the first place. My equipment may look road weary, but my sound is consistent.

I do, however, like to browse and to see what might be useful to what I'm doing. And even if I'm spending only five bucks for a set of strings, I'd rather a hometown store like Malone's gets the money and stays in business another day instead of paying some online warehouse. It's good to be able to test drive equipment and not just guess and be hopeful from pictures on the Internet. And I know if I call Johnny Malone at home at nine o'clock on a Saturday night, he'll open the store to give me anything I need in an emergency for a gig. Johnny's one of the old guard and he's a musician's friend.

Malone's is tucked between a deli and a hardware store on 7th Avenue, one of a long line of storefronts from a more prosperous era before malls and online shopping. It's easy to miss Malone's driving by if you don't know it's there. The sign out front is unpretentious and the merchandise behind the bars on the front window is carefully arranged to keep instruments out of the sun and out of the immediate reach of smash-and-grabbers from the sidewalk. Inside, the store is two floors and a basement filled with enough gear to outfit a dozen bands.

As I walked in, Nick, Johnny's clerk, jumped to his feet behind a glass display case full of effect pedals and saluted. "Hey, everybody! It's Sam Dunne, the original Old Man of the C. How you doin', dude?" He was tall and skinny, long dark hair cascading from a green fedora and tattoos snaking up both his bare arms. He was rhythmically squeezing a dirty yellow rubber ball in his left hand.

I picked up the banter gauntlet. "Still pickin' rings around your bony ass, Nick."

He started bouncing the ball on the glass countertop, passing it hand to hand. "No way, Methuselah. You were never faster than me."

"Says you," I snapped back. "When I was twenty-eight years old, you were six."

Nick cackled and nodded his head. "That's why I like you, Sam." He pointed a finger at me. "You're not like the other oldsters who come in here, take themselves so-o-o serious. You can take a joke, laugh, and throw one back that's just as good."

"It's a gift, Nick. Where's Johnny?"

He jerked his thumb to the back of the store. "In the repair room working on one of those guitars from King Tut's tomb you guys worship." He bounced the ball at me and I caught it without looking. Nick grinned. "Just checkin' your reflexes."

I bounced it back and shot him with a thumb and forefinger. I walked to the rear of the store where more than a hundred guitars in every shape and color hung from wall racks. Some kid in skater garb was trying to set a world record for the most notes played in sixty seconds. He'd shred a burst then look around to see whether anyone noticed. A new sign hung overhead: *Keep your concerts down to fifteen minutes – Management.* After the third eruption of staccato notes, I hoped this kid's fifteen was about up.

Johnny came out of the repair room with a red Gretsch Country Gentleman under one arm. "Hey, Sam, how's it going?" Johnny was about five-foot-six, stocky, and nearly bald, but he still didn't succumb to fashion and shave his head or pierce an ear. "Look at this beauty; 1962." He pulled out a shirt tail and used it to wipe of a few fingerprints off the tailpiece. He held the guitar like a proud father would hold his firstborn. His smile faded. "Hell of a thing about Eddie."

"Yeah." I ran a finger along the low E string feeling the cold roughness of the winding. "Hell of a thing. I wonder what Danny will do now, since Eddie was the musical brains of the business." Danny couldn't read a note of music and was arrogantly proud of the fact.

"Funny you should mention him. He was just here yesterday. He wanted to know if I had one of those old Rec-Tech digital 8-tracks from a few years ago. The DR-190. You bought one of those didn't you?"

"Yeah, I used it to do demos a few years back. It was a pain in the ass because it ran one of those old square Compact Flash memory cards and it made you go through a real kabuki dance to transfer individual tracks to your computer. It was built to do the mix onboard. It worked, but it ate time."

"I asked him why he'd want an oldie like that and he said he 'understood' that model – didn't like the newer ones. Too complicated, he said. Of course I don't have one, but I told him I'd keep my eyes open. He seemed a little annoyed, like I should have it here waiting for him, but you know how he is. His life should be seamless. After all, he's a star, just ask him. I don't see what the big deal is. The newer models work almost the same way as the old ones did. They still rely on memory cards, but they take SDs now. If you still have yours, there's some money to be made."

"No, it's gone. First one channel started acting squirrelly, and then another; then the pre-amp went. You know how it is with solid state gear. Everything is connected to everything and one bad circuit eventually pulls down the whole works."

Johnny nodded. "Give me an old tube amp any day."

"Besides that, even if I was starving, I wouldn't sell Danny Barton my ear wax."

"Understood." He turned to the skater and shouted over the fusillade of metal music, "Hey, Segovia, turn it down or turn it off!" He turned back to me and laughed. "I'm ready to hang a sign that says 'Free Gift Certificate to the first person who plays a whole song.' You should come in on a Saturday afternoon when all the wannabes are here. Sounds like shop class, all saws and hammers."

I laughed with him. "George Antheil would be proud, Johnny." And yes, Johnny knew the reference.

We talked guitars and amps for a while until the kid quit then we pulled a couple of acoustics off the wall and sat down to play. Playing the guitar is therapeutic. One of my old girlfriends once said that no matter how tightly wound I might be any given day, I'd sit down with a guitar and as I played, it was less like watching a flower open than watching a fist slowly uncoil.

Johnny and I worked together in a half dozen bands since high school, and jamming with him was like coming home off the road. We ran some blues and some fast shuffles, and even a few old rockers trading off finger-picking leads and chord rhythms.

The skater kid was standing around by the amps and tried to look disinterested whenever I caught him paying attention. After a few songs, he drifted over, and when we finished riffing around a standard blues in A, he said, "That's some righteous shit, man"; high praise from his generation.

That clean acoustic sound, what the guitar is really about, pushed Eddie and Kearny and Wendy Conn into the back seat. When I left, a half hour later, the world felt better to me than it did in a while.

7

The night after my interview with Kearny, I played the lounge at Casey's, a mid-sized restaurant and bar on the North side and for people my age a hideout from the twenty-somethings who drank too much, laughed too loud, and shared no context past last month. The lounge glowed with retro bar neons advertising micro beers I never heard of and rustled with conversation like leaves in the wind, barely audible over my music. I worked the room often enough that I kept a rig in their storage closet behind the bar so I wouldn't have to bother loading in and out and disturb its quiet ambiance.

Casey's lounge seats about sixty people max at the bar and the tables. The building is old and the bar is original, solid oak. The room is a tunnel, the stamped tin ceilings are high, the floor is tiled, and the wall behind the bar is a line of big mirrors, which makes EQ-ing tricky. My first time there, the microphone squealed with feedback half the night, but now I've got it figured out.

I get along well with most bar owners and managers; in fact, the only exceptions are the ones who can't get along with anybody. I'd been in the rotation at Casey's for three years, more or less, and it was the best of all worlds; close to home, early hours, and no load-in. Mark, the owner, came past as I was tuning.

Mark is a big guy with a thick mustache that matches his grey hair and an easy manner that could turn tough in a blink, a lesson that rowdy drunks learned early. "Hi, Sam."

"Wish I was. Or is it wish I were?" The subjunctive mood is a dying animal.

"Ready to rock-n-roll?" It was a running joke we shared. Rock-n-roll for his crowd in his room would be as welcome as a wet dog. People come to Casey's to kick back, not to dance; otherwise, he'd be running bands, not singles.

"Think I'll open with 'In-A-Gadda-da-Vida,' segue to 'Voodoo Child,' and cap it with an AC/DC medley. By then your crew'll be putting the chairs on the tables and mopping the floors."

Mark laughed that big booming monosyllable of his. "Sounds like a plan, Sam. Knock 'em out early and we'll all go home." He turned away and headed for the dining room.

I set my tip jar on the corner of the six-by-eight dais that served as a stage. I carry an honest-to-goodness Mason jar with me, partly because it's a conversation piece and partly because it holds more than a bar glass. I put two dollar bills in it for luck and to let people know it wasn't there as a spittoon.

The crowd was light when I started at nine, but gradually the place filled as people finished their dinners and drifted into the bar for a drink. My job was to stretch it to two drinks or three. People sneer sometimes when I refer to playing bars as a "job" or say I'm "going to work" when I leave for a gig. All I can say is, if it isn't work, why do they pay me? My job isn't to play music for three or four hours, it's to amuse drunken adults so they don't break the furniture or punch each other, and that I do well.

The first hour was okay; I've reached the point at which for that I never play a bad gig, sick, drunk, or exhausted, but most nights it's good and some nights it's better. Tonight I was a little bit off-center because of Eddie's murder and all the baggage that went with it. I ran on autopilot for a while, playing the standard mix of James Taylor, Cat Stevens, Eagles, and Billy Joel favorites with a few Gordon Lightfoot and Joni Mitchell tunes thrown in; a walk down nostalgia alley for my generation.

Gradually I loosened up as the crowd warmed to me and I started doing some of my own songs. Applause kicked in when I did "Cold Fire" and "I Can't Be Bought." Things improved from there. People wrote requests on bar napkins and stuffed bills in the jar. I shifted gears to Human Jukebox mode. Some nights I'll get twenty requests or more and play every one of them; tonight was one of those, and everything else was left on the sidewalk. In here it was only me, my guitar, and people who came to hear me.

Early into my last hour Lottie Williams showed up with her camera bag and her laptop. Lottie was an ER nurse whose hobby was photographing bands and performers at concerts, and once she got to know them better, backstage when one of the locals opened for a name act. Years ago, one of Prufrock's guys put his arm through a glass door, and she saved him from bleeding to death using a guitar strap as a tourniquet. That bought her a lifetime full-access pass from the local promoters, and gradually photography became a job as well as an avocation as she sold pictures to tabloids and magazines. Besides, it never hurt to have a trauma nurse on hand at a concert.

Lottie was a kind of mascot years ago when she was younger, and now she was more of a den mother to the bad boys and girls. In the old days she was cute and petite; these days she was still cute but built like a fireplug. Every time I saw her, her hair was a different style or color. Tonight, it was spiked, the ends tipped electric blue. On most women her age the look would have been ridiculous, but it suited her eclectic persona. I was always amazed that she found jeans that not only fit her but made her look good in spite of her build.

I finished my song and switched off the microphone. "Hey, Lottie."

"Hi, Sam. Been too long." She plopped down at a table close to the front, tilting her head and smiling. "Feelin' photogenic tonight?"

"Sure. Shoot away. You cleared it with the boss, right?" Mark tolerated nothing that disturbed the customers.

"Always. I know the drill. No noise, no flash." She started pawing through her camera bag, setting lenses and gadgets on the table.

"Lay on, MacDuff." I switched the mic back on and went into an acoustic version of "Sultans of Swing" while Lottie fitted a lens on her camera. By the time the song ended to moderate applause and a salute from the guy who requested it, Lottie was snapping away. "Should I smile?" I said aside.

Never taking her eye from the viewfinder, she said, "Just play. Leave the rest to me."

I launched into my song "Searching for a Vein." Lottie got up from her chair and started moving around the front of the room, snapping shots from different angles and distances, twirling the focus rings. She knelt to shoot upward and include the glowing Blue Moon Ale sign over my shoulder. She stood on a chair to shoot me waist up without the microphone interfering and shot from behind over my shoulder, making the crowd and the bar a backdrop; Lottie did everything but sit on my lap for a close-up. Once in a while she'd adjust the colored spotlights between shots.

In a few minutes, my music slid back into focus and she became just another part of the audience, which is how she wanted it. I was working the room pretty well, and the crowd was enjoying the show, including Lottie's paparazzi routine. A dozen songs and two encores later, it was over for that night. My gear went back in the closet, and I emptied my tip jar and sat down at Lottie's table with a bottle of Heineken.

"Nice set," she said, fiddling with her camera.

"One could say the same for you," I flirted, and we both laughed.

"Oh, you silver-tongued devil." She brought the camera up to her eye and snapped a half dozen head and shoulder pics. Then Lottie snapped what has become her trademark shot long before cell phone "selfies." She came around the table and cuddled in close to me holding her camera at arm's length to catch us both in frame. Lottie's web page is filled with pictures like it; famous faces and Lottie's happy grin.

Many years ago, Lottie and I enjoyed a quick romantic fling, saw it for what it was, and went our ways, but we stayed friends in the long term. It was always good for us, like a familiar song or a favorite old sweater; comfortable seemed the best word.

"To what do I owe the honor of this session?" I thought maybe I knew but asked anyway.

She smiled sadly. "Eddie." Lottie set the camera down and sighed. "The day he was killed, I did a shoot of him in his home studio. He called me and asked me to come over. Did you know he was planning to break with Danny and go on his own?"

I tipped my head back and let the beer pour down my throat. After a long pull I set the bottle down and raised my eyebrows. "Want one of me drinking from the bottle?" I turned it in my hand to show the label. "You know—product placement?" It stung me a little that she was suddenly interested in pixing me as an extra added attraction to Eddie. "You shoot Danny yet?"

"In a couple of days." She sensed my hurt and looked down.

"Got a buyer?" I figured she'd market the photos as a set to one of the entertainment tabloids or maybe to a newspaper for a feature article. Who knows? Maybe even *Rolling Stone*. This could be a big break for her. How could anyone blame Lottie. Neither of us was getting any younger, and like me, maybe she was thinking about growing old alone and paying bills in her golden years. Then again, maybe it wasn't about money but about recognition, legitimacy for all her years of backstage hanging on.

"Not yet, but I'll shop them around."

"Gotta be quick while it's still news; either that or wait 'til they catch the killer. As for quitting Danny, that rumor recycles every year or two. Sometimes I think they started it themselves to keep people talking."

"But this time, I think he meant it, Sam. He played a demo for me that he said would be his breakout hit. It was beautiful song, better than anything he and Danny ever wrote together. And now he's dead." Tears ran down her cheeks. She caught my look and said, "Please don't hate me, Sam."

"I could never hate you, Lottie," I said, wiping her cheek with a finger. Besides, it's just business." I leaned over and kissed her cheek and came away tasting her tears. "So, let me see what you've got."

She switched on her laptop and plugged the camera into a port. I went through another beer while she scrolled through screen after screen of my pictures. When did I start looking so old? She stopped for a minute at a close-up of my hands on the guitar, my head down. "I really like that shot, Sam. You're touching the guitar, caressing it, like it's a woman you love. That's how I like to think of you."

I was quiet for a moment. "I want a print of that one."

"You got it."

She scrolled through the last of my photos and I saw Eddie on the screen. She clicked through several and stopped at one of him smiling, leaning back against the desk in his home studio. The same thick blonde hair, the same blue eyes, and the same crooked grin that drew women like flies to a honey pot—or a garbage can. A cigarette dangled between his third finger and his pinky, the way he always held them while he Travis-picked with his other two. He looked so happy and so alive.

"Still wearing the ring, I see." On the middle finger of Eddie's right hand was his "lucky ring." I guess it wasn't so lucky after all. It was a big ugly thing he bought from some street vendor in Mexico. The ring was silver, a rattlesnake's head with the mouth open and the fangs and tongue showing. "I told him once he should have rubies put in the eyes so it would look even cheesier."

Lottie sighed. "Eddie was Eddie."

"Maybe you could print one of those for me too."

"Sure, Sam. I'd be glad to."

"Or just e-mail it, save yourself time, trouble and postage."

"I can't e-mail these files. They're too big. This is a ten-meg camera. Tell you what, if you can give me five minutes, I'll burn all yours and his onto a CD and you can pick out the ones you want me to print. It's the least I can do."

"I'd like that." As if on cue, we both leaned in for a hug. I stood up, took a last swallow from the bottle and started to the bar for another. In the pastel glow of the beer signs near the door I saw Kearny stand and throw money on the bar. Our eyes locked for a second then he gave me the one-nod, turned and walked out.

• • •

By the time I got back to my apartment, I segued from annoyed to royally pissed off. Why was Kearny following me around when it should be obvious to him that I wasn't the killer? I pulled back the edge of the curtain and peered out the third floor window at the end of the hallway. No unmarked car idling at the curb; no figure in the shadows with the glowing tip of a cigarette. I listened at the stairwell; no furtive footsteps. Then I was angry with myself, too. I was falling for Kearny's cop act, letting it rattle me for no reason and spoil an otherwise good night. I was innocent, but Kearny was making me feel guilty.

When I shut my apartment door, I usually leave the world and all its crap outside. Tonight that didn't work. Years ago I got past Gin Sing and lost opportunities, but Eddie's murder and its fallout brought the whole thing back. I dropped Lottie's CD on the desk with my car keys and headed for the kitchen. Time for supper: a microwaved ham and cheese sandwich with one more beer. This was number four, one past my usual self-imposed limit, but tonight I didn't worry about it.

I ate my late night meal in the living room in front of the television set. Subscribing to cable or some satellite network seemed unnecessary, so I opted for the digital box. It's better to have a dozen free channels I never watch than two hundred pay channels I never watch. Tonight I switched between Leno and Letterman to see what musical acts might be on. Watching the two of them try frantically to stay hip and relevant while the edge drifts out of reach is painful, and I saw myself in their desperation. I nodded off before one o'clock and woke the next morning still in the armchair, stiff and hung over.

Another day in paradise.

I ran the shower from hot to cold and shaved with lukewarm water as the heater recovered. Chores were waiting. Bookkeeping for my tax accountant occupied most of the morning. A lesson learned decades ago: to make a living in the music business, get up at the same time every day and go to work. That work may be writing songs, calling venues, recording demos, knocking on doors, promoting yourself, whatever; gigs are overtime. Sleep past noon every day and soon you'll be hitchhiking back to Keokuk, Iowa disillusioned and broke.

Somehow, I pulled it off day to day, although as I got older and as people who knew my songs from Gin Sing thinned out, it was harder to land new gigs and at times to hold onto the established ones. Younger crowds want younger entertainment. Joe Mancini, my agent, regularly pestered Re-Mark Music, a promoter that packaged tours of older talent to second-string theaters, to put me in their lineup. If people would pay to see Gary Puckett and the Union Gap and The Syndicate of Sound, there might be a place on the bill for me. I'd even take a slot as a sideman; I knew all of the songs. Another good bet would be the casinos that sprung up over the last ten years in Pennsylvania. Joe was perpetually "working on it," but I understood that I was fast approaching the point at which I just wasn't an attraction any more. Lottie's photos didn't lie any more than the mirror.

After lunch, I sat down to brainstorm on lyrics. Songwriting, like the rest of the music business, has always been a right-place-right-time circumstance. Putting the right melody with the right words with the right band doesn't guarantee a hit. The public has to buy it, and although the Business with a Capital B has the process pretty well formulized, the public is still the arbiter of what hits and what doesn't. If we knew what people really wanted week to week, we'd all be rich.

In the meantime, we songwriters plod along, guitar under one arm and laptop under the other in search of a combination of tune and words that at least stands a chance. Today it was a hook that rattled around my head for months before I decided to put it on paper. Like most of my songs, I try to find a simple line that states an undeniable truth in a new way and tie it to a story. If the listener is hooked by the tag line and can identify with the narrative, the song has a better than average shot. If the melody has a good musical hook as well, the odds improve, but it's still a crapshoot.

A long-term relationship ended for me when the woman at the other end decided that the best way to deal with the breakup was to simply hang up the phone and refuse to talk, although she still loved me. I guess these days you don't actually "hang up" a cell phone, although the phrase persists.

I typed, "You can hang up the phone, but you can't hang up on your heart." Not bad for a tag line, but not quite right. Anyone who teaches writing can tell you that the second-person "you" grabs people, but like hooking a fish, it's not enough; you have to make listeners identify with the characters in the song to set the hook and reel them in.

I changed the tag to "You can hang up on me, but you can't hang up on your heart." Much better; both first- and second-person are involved. Most

people have been on one side of a breakup or the other and experienced
the frustration that happens on either side. "You can hang up on me" plays
to both, and male or female, a listener can see himself or herself in one
of the roles. "Visualize" is the word of choice on Madison Avenue. "But
you can't hang up on your heart" adds a third-person element, closes the
triangle; you, me, it. Personalities aside, some truths can't be denied—hey,
that rhymes and has rhythm—and the metaphor of hanging up on the
heart, trying to elude something inescapable, forges a solid image.

"Even though you can't hear me, my love will ring in your –" I can't say
"heart" again. What do I rhyme with heart? "You can hang up on me, but
you can't hang up on your heart." Not there yet, but on the path.

I reached for the rhyming dictionary: art, cart, dart, fart, hart, mart
part, tart; two syllables: apart. Yeah. "Our love will ring and you'll feel it
although we're apart." I'll run with that for now. The double entendre of
"ring" including the context of the telephone and some resounding force
works well. I'm not so sure about "feel" rather than "hear", but it undercuts
the expectation in a line involving sound and tying in an emotion. "Our
love still rings . . ." Too stilted; too hard to sing fluidly. The present tense
makes for a sense of here and now, but the future tense suggests continuity.
"Will ring" it is.

After hours of staring at the screen, my eyeballs start to ache, and it's
time to quit, but I made a good start on the new song. I saved the file and
checked my e-mail. The Community College wanted me for a night class
in the spring term. Monday and Wednesday 7:00 to 8:15; Mondays are
usually dead, and I could still do Wednesday gigs in town from 9:00 to
midnight if they're close by. It could work. They gave me a week before the
offer turned into a pumpkin, so I wrote myself a reminder on a Post-it to
check the dates with Joe and stuck it on the corner of my screen.

Near the end of the New Mail queue was an assignment from the essay
mill for a ten-page research paper on "Facades in *The Great Gatsby*." That
meant some quick bucks. I could write that one in my sleep.

I fixed myself an early supper. Remembering Wendy's crack about my
arteries, I opted for healthful: grilled tilapia with three peppers and lemon
sauce with rice pilaf. It usually tastes great with a beer, but I planned on
working out later in the evening, and if I waited for the food to settle, a
beer would put me to sleep before I could hit the gym. I pulled a bottle of
water out of the fridge and applauded my restraint.

9

I rolled into The Pumphouse around seven thirty and the usual crowd was there. Wednesday is my night to work legs. I was in the middle of my stretches when one of the cocky young hard bodies, a twenty-something named Teddy strolled over. He was a bully with a bad steroid complexion and a lot of mouth. He benched three-fifty and made sure everybody knew it. I'd seen him around the gym and didn't like him, though I'd never talked to him in my life. I had the impression he didn't like me much either. Most people get along with most people, but we all find a few whose personalities from the first look just seem to meet ours at right angles. Teddy was one of mine. I saw him say something over his shoulder to his pals and they all looked my way and laughed.

I was doing deep knee bends and he waited to step over until I was down in a squat so that his crotch was level with my face. "You're Sam Dunne, huh?" He looked at me out of the bottom of his eyes.

I straightened to a standing position and fronted him. "You have to ask? Sounds like you know already."

Teddy was about three inches taller and thirty pounds heavier than I was. He was wearing a black Gold's Gym T-shirt with the arm holes and the neck torn to accommodate his bulk. He folded his arms across his chest to show off his triceps. "Well, some of the guys were talking and they said you used to play in the band with that dude got killed." Bullies always find the sore spot; poke and provoke.

I stared him down. "That 'dude' had a name: Eddie Shay." A little more edge crept into my tone than I expected.

"Yeah, so?"

"He was an okay guy. Now he's a dead guy. You talk about him, you show some respect." The kid's attitude was pissing me off, and I was growing one to match it. I didn't like Eddie much, but I liked Teddy even less.

Teddy's grin turned into a sneer. "Hey, old man, don't get loud on me. Anyway, he was just some cokehead from what I hear. Besides, I think you're a little bit grey to be tellin' me how to behave." The music still boomed in the background, but suddenly the weights stopped clanking as if some subliminal signal went off, and everybody stared at us. I pulled a fifty pound barbell plate off the rack and held it chest height at three and nine o'clock to put it on the squat machine. I smiled at him. "You're probably right. All I can say is—catch!" I threw the plate at his chest and he managed to snag it with both hands, but it tipped him backwards over a bench and onto the floor.

I jumped the bench, put my heel in his solar plexus, and looked down into a face full of startled fear. "I'm stepping outside now and I'll stand right in front of that window so you can see where I am. You want to discuss Eddie Shay further, come on out." My eyes swept the room. "And bring your friends." I took an empty curling bar off the rack, swung it once in a wide arc like a samurai sword, and carried it out the door.

I stood on the sidewalk in the chill night air staring through the front window of the gym until Brian, the owner came outside. He was my height with an extra fifty pounds of muscle and a round, shaved head that looked like a tomato in the neon light from the gym sign. We went back a long time. "I think you made your point, Sam. Teddy and his two buddies ducked out the emergency exit about ten minutes ago. If they haven't come around front yet, I don't imagine they will. If they did, I'd've been out here too, and a few more of the guys. We've been watching it. Hell, I'm glad Denzel isn't here. He would've broken that punk's legs for him." He held out his hand for the bar.

I handed it to him. "Sorry, Brian. I guess I'm touchier about Eddie than I thought. I never expected to see a day when I'd stick up for him. Like my old man used to say, Eddie was a dog, but he was my dog. Maybe I'd better go someplace else to lift from now on."

He shook his head. "Nah. Give it a week. You scared Teddy and his pals enough that I doubt it'll happen again, but I can't just let it go. For what it's worth, as many people respect you for it as don't. Come on back in and finish your workout." He laughed. "Just don't kill anybody. It's bad for my insurance."

I did squats until my legs ached and then I did some more. Sweat ran in my eyes and they stung so much I couldn't keep them open. I could barely walk to the van when I was done. I looked around the parking lot for Teddy and his pals. They were nowhere to be seen, but I was too tired to be disappointed.

"Just don't kill anybody."

10

My cell phone woke me. The alarm clock read 7:12. "I flicked the phone open in the dark bedroom and squinted with one eye at the bright screen. "This building better be on fire."

"Sam, it's Wendy Conn. Turn on Channel Seven, quick."

"Huh?"

"Channel Seven. Now. Just do it." The phone clicked in my ear.

I almost rolled over and went back to sleep, but the urgency in her voice nudged me out of bed. I stumbled across the living room and found the remote on the coffee table. The TV came on and I punched in Seven just in time to hear Donna Fields, *Jumpstart's* blonde co-host say, "—and after these messages, Danny Barton will sing his new tribute to his late band mate and fellow song writer Eddie Shay. We'll be right back."

While the commercials ran, I put a blank DVD in the recorder. Roto-Rooter, the Geico Gecko, We Buy Any Car, and back to *Jumpstart*. Donna Fields looked into the camera with rehearsed sincerity, reading from a teleprompter, and said, "We all mourn the loss of one of our local stars, Gin Sing's Eddie Shay, whose murder remains unsolved, but few mourn that loss more than Eddie's partner in song, band mate and co-writer, Sunsong recording artist Danny Barton."

The camera pulled back. Donna Fields and her ever-dapper co-host Trey Smith were perched on high stools; between them on a third stool Danny Barton posed with an acoustic guitar, arms around it from behind like I might hug a girlfriend. He wore a black blazer over jeans and a white linen shirt. The years weren't much kinder to him than they were to me. A pair of tinted wire-rims perched on his nose, almost hiding crow's feet and the pouches under his eyes. His graying hair cascaded over his shoulders and his beard was trimmed in that annoying length that suggests he just started growing it last week although he sported one for twenty years.

Trey Smith picked up the ball. "And in memory of his friend and collaborator, Danny Barton has written a new song, and he's going to perform it for us now. How were you able to write a song so quickly, especially as overwrought as you must be over Eddie's death?"

A second camera caught Danny knees to head as he said, "The song just came to me a couple of days ago, and I think it's the way Eddie would want everyone to remember him. I hope this will keep him in their hearts. It's called 'Carry On'."

Danny shifted the guitar to his knee and began an arpreggiated riff in a soft rock mode. It sounded a little harsh because he was playing with a pick—finger style never worked as well for him as it did for Eddie or for me—but some of that harshness could be blamed on the sound techs in the booth. He began to sing and I was surprised at how well his voice held up.

The song was lyrical, a really nice melody that would lend itself to harmony, and with a good arrangement behind it, the song would sell. The lyrics weren't bad. They were maudlin, not quite up to Danny's standard, but in the context of Eddie's death and the brief time span, that would be overlooked by civilians. A thoughtful edit would fix the problem. The director had a good eye. He pulled the camera back to show Eddie and an adoring Donna who looked as if she wanted to jump his bones right there.

The song ended, and after an appropriate silence, Donna said, "That was beautiful. I can see how much Eddie's loss touched you."

Danny nodded somberly. "Yes, I think I understand how Paul McCartney must have felt when John Lennon died." I almost threw an empty Rolling Rock bottle through the TV screen.

The moment over, Trey was back in the party. "And we understand you have special plans for the proceeds from this song?"

"I hope to use the royalties from 'Carry On' to start a scholarship program in Eddie's name to encourage and foster young songwriters so that they can carry on in Eddie's footsteps."

"A noble goal," said Trey to the camera. "Danny Barton of Gin Sing with his new song in memory of Eddie Shay, 'Carry On.' Best of luck to you with the new song, Danny, and we'll carry on with *Jumpstart* after these messages."

I stared unseeing at the television as the commercials rolled on.

My cell phone rang. "It's Wendy. Comment?"

"Jesus! Don't you ever let up?"

"Hey, just messin' with you."

"No you weren't. That really pisses me off, somebody says something sharp and when the other person gets ticked, she says, 'Just messin' with you, dude,' as if that makes it okay or something. It doesn't. You said it. I'm pissed."

"Okay, okay. Sorry. Take it easy."

"And that ticks me off too," I went on, my voice rising. "You crank somebody up, and then when it looks like he might take your head off, just say, 'Take it easy. Calm down. Relax. Chill, dude. Switch to decaf.' When

I'm pissed off, I don't want to calm down—oh, hell—this whole thing hit me the wrong way. And if you quote that, I'll hunt you down and – pour my decaf in your goddamned laptop."

A short silence, then Wendy said, "Well then, how about breakfast?" as if I'd never raised my voice. I laughed in spite of myself.

"You're good."

"So I'm told. Dora's in an hour?"

"Can't this morning. How about tomorrow?"

"Won't work for me. Saturday?

"Okay, Saturday."

"Your turn to buy."

"What happened to the expense account?"

"Saturday's my day off." She laughed that smoky laugh of hers and hung up.

I played "Carry On" one more time, closing my eyes and listening to the melody. It needed polish, but unless I missed something, Danny had a hit in the hopper, especially riding on Eddie's death and all the publicity it would generate. I felt a little bit envious then shook it off, remembering I'd have to be Danny to do the things he did, and that was one skin I didn't want to live in. Mine was a tough enough proposition.

After a quick bowl of Frosted Flakes—I regretted passing on Dora's pancakes—I spent the morning pounding out the essay about facades; Gatsby's feigned legitimacy, Tom and Daisy's thinly veiled matrimonial discord, and the lack of pretense on Wilson's part because he's just a poor working stiff. The more money you have, the easier it is to erect and maintain a false front, and the more likely people will accept it as reality, if from nothing more than deference to power. Art mirrors life; no façades for me—no money.

I went online to the HACC Library. One worthwhile perk of working for HACC was almost unlimited library privileges. In about fifteen minutes I had the requisite eight sources for the paper; six of them full text from ProQuest. I finished a draft of the essay in about two hours, saved it on the drive, and printed a copy. Not my best work, but it would buy some rich kid a B plus and help him (or her) maintain the façade of a good student. I'd let it sit for a day then proofread it and clean it up. Everything looks good when you pull it out of the printer. It isn't until a day or so later that you can read it and realize that a few things you thought you wrote are missing in action.

That night I switched on the television while I got dressed for the evening to catch the local news. The flap about Eddie's murder had run its course for the time being. The newspapers carried reports of an ongoing investigation on the inside pages. The TV news moved on to more immediate events for its lead stories. One thing the news never exhausts is tragedy; there's a new one every day.

Thursday night I played my regular gig at Mike and Kelli's, a small bar and grille tucked between an insurance agency and a chiropractor's office. The owners—can you guess their names?—took a chance and bought the place from Benny Laszlo's widow last year. Mike and Kelli Peck are struggling because of the bum economy and the everyday perils of a small business, so I come in to play for a few hours every week to try to attract some trade for them and work for a nominal amount of money. I could make much more elsewhere, but I like Mike and Kelli; they work hard, and I want them to succeed. Somebody asked me once why I don't just play there for free. The answer is simple. If they pay me what I ask, it isn't charity, and they keep their dignity. Besides, Kelli makes the best Reuben in town.

Mike and Kelli's seats twenty at the bar and has café tables with tall sidewalk stools along one wall and lower dining tables along another. It's small, a friendlier word might be intimate, and I've never come in to find the place empty. I attribute that to the Mike and Kelli's personalities as much as the food.

"Sam I am!" yelled Kelli from behind the bar. I made a big show of eyeballing the menu chalked on a slate near the door. "I don't see green eggs and ham," I said. She shot back, "Only for special customers."

I set up in my corner under a glitter-coated cardboard star Mike hung from the ceiling, as he put it (without irony) "in recognition of your status." He brought me a ginger ale with lots of ice and set it beside me. He was a thin guy, Jack Spratt to his buxom blonde wife, and over the last year, he never lost his optimistic grin. "How's business, Mike?"

He laughed. "Well, I'm not ordering my Mercedes this week, but we're paying the bills."

"Keep the grille warm. I want a Reuben and fries when I'm done."

"Will do."

Seven people sat at the bar, most of them watching the television for the daily Lottery numbers, and three of the tables had couples. I always waited until the numbers were drawn to start playing; I agree with Ambrose Bierce's definition of the lottery: "a tax on people bad at math," but I respect others' vices. Once the groans and ticket tearing ritual were done, Mike turned off the TV, I kicked on my amp, and the evening officially began.

Two of the couples were regulars who came every Tuesday for drinks and to hear me play, according to Mike. The other couple was new; a middle-aged pair who sat across from each other like bookends, eating Kelli's special as if it were a duty. Some people just don't appreciate fine bar cuisine.

I did my usual run of covers while the happy hour gang at the bar drifted out in ones and twos and were replaced by the serious drinkers on the second shift. These were regulars too, most of them loners who came in, as Jenny put it, for "faces and voices." Kelli summed it up best: "We're a living room that they don't have to clean up."

Applause comes in spurts in Mike and Kelli's. I don't expect it after every song, but I know the crowd is listening. I see feet tapping on the rungs of the bar stools and the subtle dance of bottles and glasses as hands rock in rhythm lets me know we're on the same page. As I reached for my drink, I saw a group of women come in. They were in their late twenties to mid- thirties, loud and laughing. Mike and Kelli's wasn't their first stop of the evening and probably wouldn't be the last. The eight of them pulled tables together and generally took over the place.

I figured them for a gang of co-workers. They were dressed in upscale office casual and ranged in looks from plain to knockout. "Evening, ladies," I boomed through the microphone. "What's the happy occasion?"

"Tess got a promotion," one of them yelled, and the others cheered and clapped. Tess, a tall brunette, raised her arms in a victor's pose. Nothing shy about her.

I had to hook them early or compete with them the rest of the night. I know better than to ask a single patron who's the center of attention, "What song do you want to hear?" in case I couldn't play it. Instead, I said, "Congratulations, Tess. This one's for you." I fired up "I Can't be Bought" and leered at the girls at key points in the lyrics. "I can't be bought, but I can be stolen, on a moonlight night when your libido's swollen. I can be very entertainin' once I get rollin.' Just have me home before the church bell's tollin.'"

It worked. We were all friends for the evening. The girls poured pitchers of margaritas, gobbled nachos and dispensed with the formality of written requests, shouting them out song after song. I played most of them or at least a tune by the same artist to cheers and clapping. Then one of them yelled, "Do you know Gin Sing? Play 'Cry for me Mama!'" That stopped me cold. They didn't realize who I was. I didn't say anything for a half a minute. As a rule, I play only the Gin Sing songs that I wrote, but I took a deep breath started "Cry for me Mama," thinking, don't derail the train. Mike and Kelli, this one's for you.

I played an hour longer than usual, and I'd guess the bar did about three times its normal trade that night. I knocked off around ten as the office party was breaking up with girl hugs and air kisses. I sat at the bar and had a beer while Kelli made my sandwich. She brought it in a bag. "What's this?"

"I figured you'd want it to go." She pointed with her chin. I turned on my stool and saw one of the office gang sitting alone at the table. She smiled. I smiled back. She wasn't the best looker in the bunch, but she wasn't the worst, either. Sometimes you win one.

12

Kearny called me Friday morning. "Something's come up. I need to talk with you. Can you come in?"

"It's not exactly convenient right now."

"Well, we could come to you…"

The subtle shift from "I" to "we" set off alarms. The thought of Kearny bringing a couple of cops with him to my apartment and them separating like a team of shoplifters wandering around a store so that you can't watch them all at once felt like a real threat. I didn't have anything illegal at my place, but who knew what they might leave behind?

"Not necessary. What time do you want me there?"

"As soon as you can make it."

"I'll be down in a half hour."

At the station, Kearny reduced the twenty-minute wait to five. He was wearing a different suit today, the twin of the tan one in navy blue, but the same striped tie. "C'mon back, Sam." He led me down the hallway toward the interrogation room where we'd sat last time, but we passed it and kept moving toward a push bar door at the end. "Where are we going?"

"I need to show you something." We took the stairs to the basement parking level where an unmarked car waited.

Kearny opened the passenger door. "Let's take a ride." Neither of us spoke. Kearny was working his anxiety routine, and I kept quiet, waiting to see where it led. It led four blocks to the parking area of the City Morgue. Without looking at me, Kearny got out of the car and said, "C'mon."

I'd been at the morgue once before to identify Tinker Ross, a drummer who overdosed on downers. The place creeped me out then, and it creeped me out now. The paunchy security guard at the garage entrance waved us past, and Kearny led me through a maze of corridors to what the cops jokingly called the "File Room."

The room smelled of antiseptic and cold. I couldn't see my breath in the air, but it felt as if I should. Overhead, glaring fluorescent lights shone on a polished terrazzo floor. One of the lights buzzed like a trapped fly. A skinny white-coated attendant with a face like a ferret and a hatless uniformed sergeant with a name tag that said McKinley were waiting for us. McKinley was telling a joke, and the attendant was laughing just a little too loudly. Minus one for decorum, but I guess when you work with dead bodies all day, you need to remind yourself once in a while that you're a live one.

Against two opposing walls, cadaver drawers stood in ranks. "We'd like you to help us I.D. someone. " Kearny nodded to the attendant who pulled out a drawer. An off-kilter wheel clicked in the track as the drawer slid from its niche. Kearny gestured with his head for me to stand beside him.

He pulled back the sheet—blue spiked hair. It was Lottie. He flipped the sheet down to her waist. Lottie had a dragon tattooed on her left breast. I saw a puckered hole through the dragon's head and another just under her rib cage.

Kearny said matter-of-factly, "She didn't show up for work yesterday, didn't answer her phone. The neighbors heard her stereo on, couldn't get her to answer the door, so the super went in and found her."

I felt my stomach heave and I bent double, vomiting on the marble. I gulped for air, then I straightened up and snarled, "You sonofabitch..." I spun on the balls of my feet and decked Kearny with a left to his jaw. Before I could pounce on him, McKinley and the attendant grabbed me by the arms and pinned me against the cold steel of the drawers. McKinley pulled a sap. He flicked a questioning eyebrow at Kearny, who pushed himself up with one hand as he raised the other in a "stop" gesture. "No! Don't hit him."

Kearny stood up. He rubbed his jaw and looked me in the face. "Understand something. I've got two homicides in two weeks, and you're the common element. I needed to get you here before this made the news. You were right to hit me. That was a shitty thing for me to do, but this was my only way to know what I need to know, and now I do. Are you going to swing at me again?"

"No," I hissed through clenched teeth.

He told the guys holding me, "Let him go," and said to me, "Now let's go find the bastard who did this."

● ● ●

Back at the Precinct in the interrogation room, Kearny sat on one side of the table holding a can of Mountain Dew from the break room vending machine against his face. "I have a real problem, Sam. I'm stumped by all this. Last time you were here, you were, shall we say, less than cooperative. Maybe now that you have a reason to help me you will."

I glared at him. "That's why you pulled the surprise with Lottie? To shock me into helping you?"

He shook his head. "No, I figured once you knew she was dead, no matter how you found out, you'd want to see the killer nailed. I needed to be sure you didn't know anything about it."

"And now you are sure?"

"As sure as I can be under the circumstances."

"Do you want to hear my alibi?"

"You play Mike and Kelli's every Thursday, right?"

"Yep, and I was there last night, even played an hour over. And if I really have to, I can give you the name of a lady who can tell you what I was doing 'til the wee hours, unless she's embarrassed, and in that case, she'll at least tell you where I was."

He nodded and shifted gears, pushing a file across the table. "I don't know dick about music except what I like to hear. I want you to look at some crime scene photos and tell me if anything looks wrong, out of place."

I frowned. "At Lottie's?" I hadn't been in Lottie's apartment since a party a couple of years before.

"No, Eddie's."

It seems that everyone who plays an instrument has a home studio now that computers and digital music make it possible and affordable. I'd never been in Eddie's studio, never been in his house for that matter, so I was seeing it all for the first time.

Eddie Shay's home studio was a long room. The floor was tongue and groove hardwood, oak from the look of it, and the walls were covered on three sides with grey textured foam to absorb unwanted noise and echoes. Everything else was white. The dropped ceiling was standard acoustical tile in a grid. Instead of building booths, Eddie opted for portable acoustic panels on casters. Based on what I saw, he was working it on the cheap. Gin Sing made money, but not as much as people thought they did. Or maybe Eddie blew it on wine, women, and wardrobe. The studio seemed more a place to develop ideas than produce a finished product, although people could work miracles with the right gear and software.

Various workstations ringed the room. One had a Yamaha synthesizer hooked to a desktop computer, another, a full set of drums ringed with mikes. A third area had amplifiers and a half-dozen guitars and basses in a floor rack like the bicycle stations you see at the library.

At the near end was Eddie's favorite, his old gold Gibson Les Paul. Eddie's desk and a table with power amps, mixers, and monitor speakers stood at the other end of the room.

Eddie's studio was tidier than most I've seen. Cables snaked across the floor from one end to the other taped down in neat bundles. Others hung like lariats from hooks on the walls alongside headphones and patch cords. In the middle of the floor was a dark stain.

"I could have done without seeing that one," I said, flipping it face down. "That's almost as bad as looking at Lottie."

Kearny nodded. "See anything unusual?" His matter-of-fact attitude pissed me off a little bit, but I suppose that when your job is to deal with brutality every day even murder becomes mundane.

"I can't really tell from these pictures. I've never been in the place, so I don't know if things have been taken or moved."

"How about this one?" Kearny tapped a finger on a print that showed the top of Eddie's desk. The desk was cluttered with papers and office junk; a stapler, a skull mug full of pens and pencils, a spindle of CDs, and a half empty box of Snickers bars, Eddie's favorite snack. Guitar picks, a set of D'Addario light gauge strings and a pair of capos were scattered among the other items. A closed laptop rested on one corner.

I leaned back in the chair, massaging my eyes with the tips of my fingers. "Did you look at the laptop?"

"The lab cracked it. Nothing important any of us could see, but just like this room, I don't know what I'm looking for. Maybe you could take a look."

I nodded, thinking that to do so would be like digging up Eddie's corpse and rooting through his bones. "I could do that. How about the CDs? Anything on them?"

"Blanks."

"Maybe he stored his work someplace else safe from a fire or a break-in, but you'd think he'd have at least a few with data on them. The *Sentinel* articles mentioned a girlfriend who was staying with Eddie on and off; she might know where he hid them."

Kearny nodded. "Lisa Barnes. She has an alibi. She was conveniently out of town the night of the murder."

"Not too convenient for Eddie," I said. "If she'd been there, he might still be alive."

"Or she might be dead too. We questioned her, but that business about the disks never came up. She said he didn't allow her in his studio; called it his," he shuffled through his notes, "his *sanctum sanctorum* or some crap like that."

"The holy of holies. Yeah, Eddie would have seen it that way; the magic temple where the Muses come to play."

"Muses?"

"The Muses were Ancient Greek goddesses who inspired artists, poets, composers, all creative people."

"Sounds like he had a pretty big ego, what with a pipeline to the gods, and all that."

"You have no idea." Eddie's ego was the size of the Moon. Most rock star egos rest uneasy on their pinnacles, hoping their brass and bravado will keep them in place one more day as the winds of public adoration shift. The only person I knew with an ego larger yet less deserved was Danny Barton.

I looked again at the photo of Eddie's desk. On top of the pile of papers was a familiar item, a blank Library of Congress "PA," Performing Arts form to register a copyright for a song. The corner of a second form showed behind the first. I pointed them out to Kearny. "Copyright forms. Eddie was always very protective of the songs he and Danny wrote. He didn't trust the Internet to submit his copyrights in digital form for fear some hacker might steal his work, so he used hard copy—paper forms. They cost almost twice as much to process, but he felt safer with them than sending an e-form."

"Is that important?"

"If anything, it's consistent, not different. It means Eddie was working on songs and planning to copyright them; business as usual."

"Damn. I hoped that might have meant something."

The single picture of the recording equipment was cursory. The photographer didn't assign much importance to the area, since it was away from the body. "Were there fingerprints on any of this stuff?"

"Apart from Eddie Shay's and Danny Barton's there are some unidentified prints on some of the guitars and other instruments, but not many; no matches on them yet."

I nodded. "That would be consistent too. He was always careful about who he let in the studio; more paranoia about people stealing his songs or his ideas." It occurred to me that Johnny Malone may be the source of the odd prints, since he did all of Eddie's guitar maintenance, but I kept that thought to myself. "So you printed Danny Barton?"

Kearny nodded. "Yeah, he came in right away and gave us his prints— very cooperative. He was pretty torn up about Eddie's death."

I'm sure he cooperated. The last thing Danny wanted was the cops running unidentified prints from the crime scene and finding they matched his on file in the AFI System for a drug charge from years ago. That little event was lost and forgotten in the general memory, and he didn't want it coming back to haunt him.

"Makes sense," I said. "Without Eddie, I'd say he's pretty much done. Eddie was the real genius between the two of them. Danny wrote some good lyrics, but Eddie was the melody man. You said you found prints on the guitars; how about the recording equipment?"

"Only Shay's."

"That figures too. He wouldn't let other people mess with his songs. No prints from the girlfriend?"

Kearny shook his head. "Nope."

I flipped through the photos one more time. "I'm sorry. I really can't tell you much more from those pictures. "

"Actually, you've told me a lot." Kearny shuffled the crime scene pix back into their folder.

"Maybe I could spot something unusual if I saw the place in person. Could we do that?"

Kearny thought about it for a minute then nodded. "I'll get it cleared; probably not 'til after tomorrow." He hesitated. "There's one more." He pushed a print, face down, toward me. I knew what it was before he said, "I hate to do this to you twice in one day, Sam."

I flipped the print over. It was Eddie belly up on the studio floor. Sometimes you read about faces of the dead looking peaceful or looking twisted in fear or agony, but Eddie's was totally blank. Even his hard-wired ironic smirk was gone, like an erased cassette. A dark patch spread from the placket of his shirt. By his head, I could see a small pile of white powder. His emptied wallet lay open beside him. My eyes moved to his hands. The left was palm up, the right palm down across his waist, as if he'd been playing a guitar and someone had taken it from him. "He's not wearing his ring."

Kearny leaned forward. "What ring?"

"Eddie always wore what he called his 'lucky' ring, the snake head, on his right hand. You remember the cover for Gin Sing's LP *Punch Drunk*? The cover was mostly Eddie's fist with that big freakin' ring."

Kearny nodded slowly. "I remember that cover. You say he always wore the ring?"

"He wore it all the time when I was in the band, and the damned thing was on his finger every time I saw him since."

Kearny pulled a sheet from the file and scanned through it quickly. "No ring in the personal effects when he came into the morgue."

"Maybe it's in the house somewhere."

"That I don't know. Between the CDs and the ring, maybe it's time to look the whole place over again."

I got up to leave. "Watch yourself, Sam," Kearny said, opening the door. "First Eddie, then Lottie; you might be next on somebody's wish list."

"Why? I don't know anything."

Kearny eyelids drooped and he gave me a three-count. "But he doesn't know you don't know."

I was almost out the door when I turned and said to Kearny, "Did you search Lottie's place?"

Kearny nodded. "Not much to see."

"Find any coke?"

"Nah. Just a little bag of grass in a dresser drawer and some prescription sleepers. No hard stuff."

"That sounds right. Did you check her camera?"

Kearny's eyes narrowed. "Yeah, there were two of them. Why?"

"You were there when she shot the pics of me at Casey's. If it's okay, I'd like to have them for promo, and for sentimental reasons."

"They came up empty. Nothing on the cards."

"Maybe they're on her laptop or she burned them onto disks. Could your lab guys keep an eye out?"

Kearny thought it over, giving me that one lip over the other thing. "I'll see what I can do."

"Thanks." On the way out the front door I decided I never wanted to play poker with Mike Kearny. Wendy, either. No pictures of Eddie on Lottie's camera. Either Kearny was holding out on me, or the killer erased them. If so, something on that camera got Lottie killed. I wouldn't tell Kearny about her pictures from Eddie's studio for a while. I wanted to compare them to what I saw in the cop shots first.

In *I, the Jury,* Mike Hammer tells his police counterpart that the race is on between them to find the guy who killed his friend. I wasn't Mike Hammer, but I wasn't throwing down the glove to Kearny, either. Evidence gets lost, arresting officers make mistakes, and killers sometimes walk. I wanted to be sure, for Lottie, and for Eddie; maybe for myself, too. Once I was certain, somebody's bill would come due, and from that moment, I knew whose it would be.

In the photo of the table full of recording gear was a thin, flat box, black with drawbars and knobs, about twelve inches by eighteen. I glossed over it at first, thinking it was just a mixer, but then I realized what it was. It was an eight-track digital recorder, and unless I was mistaken, it was a Rec-Tech DR 109.

13

That night I flopped on the sofa with a beer and switched on the local news in time to see Lottie's picture flash onto the screen. "—local nurse who was found shot to death in her apartment yesterday. Lucinda Williams is the apparent victim of a home invasion." An elderly neighbor in a flowered housecoat who didn't bother to put in her teeth said that Lottie—she called her Lottie, not Lucinda—was a sweet girl and a good neighbor. "I just can't believe she's dead." Believe it, lady. I've seen the body.

"Police are asking anyone with information concerning the crime to call the Crime Stopper Hotline at the number you see on the screen. In other news, City Council has voted to appropriate…"

I thumbed off the TV set and stared at the blank screen. Sixty seconds was all she got, and no mention of her photography. Nothing but the facts, ma'am.

I booted my computer. Plenty of spam was waiting on my e-mail plus a second notice about the comp class from HACC. I'd have to make a decision on that one soon.

I put Lottie's CD in the drive. Because she downloaded the files directly from her camera, the directory was a long list of numbered jpeg files. I clicked on the first one and Eddie smiled over his guitar from the screen. One by one, I clicked through the images looking for the one I wanted. More than fifty shots in, I found the pic of Eddie leaning against the desk. Lottie's focus was sharp, but the focus was Eddie, not the details of the room. I could probably count Eddie's eyelashes, but not the pencils in the mug. I found six of those shots from different angles, and in each case, I couldn't see the details of the desk clearly.

I'm okay with the computer when it comes to music and e-mail, but that's about the limit of my expertise. I would need some help to find out what I wanted to know.

The phone rang. It was Wendy. "I hear you've got a mean left hook."

"Been talkin' to Kearny, huh?"

"Not just him, that story's all over the precinct. So you knew Lucinda Williams, the nurse who was killed."

"Everybody knew Lottie. She was our favorite photographer. " I added, "And she was my friend."

"Some people at the paper knew her too. The Arts section used some of her photos once in a while. That's sad. It must shake you a little bit, losing two people you know that close together."

"You're right about that," I admitted before I caught myself. "So, I guess you're covering Lottie's murder too, right?" An edge crept into my voice. "Did you call me for a comment?"

"No, no comment." She sounded a little stung. "I just called to see how you're holding up."

"I'm not on suicide watch yet, but if that changes, I'll give you an exclusive."

Wendy said something that was interrupted by a click on the line. "Gotta go; the office is beeping in. See you tomorrow at eight-thirty. Take care of yourself, Sam." She hung up. I wondered how many meaningful things go unsaid because of Call Waiting and headed for the fridge for another beer.

"Did you call me for a comment?"

14

I woke up before the alarm Saturday and looked out the window. Early morning sun made the world look reasonable and for a minute I forgot what a snake pit it turned into over the last week. I decided the night before that if I was right about Danny, I needed help. Wendy was the likeliest candidate; she had an ear in the police department and I could pull her in with the potential for a career-making exclusive. I had to play it right, not too much, not too fast. Today I'd find out whether she'd play at all.

Out of the shower, I pulled on jeans and buttoned an old denim Fur Peace Ranch shirt over a red tee. I looked in the mirror and thought I might run a brush through my hair again then questioned my motives. "What you see is what you get, honey," I said to the mirror. I slipped on my jacket and slipped out the door.

Dora's was busy as always, but I stopped at the counter to say hello to Jenny. She has the unnerving ability to carry on a conversation and maintain eye contact while she fills a coffee cup without even looking at it, never spilling a drop. Today she was filling six cups on a tray.

"How do you do that?"

She grinned. The Lauren Hutton gap between her front teeth was more attractive that I wanted to admit. What do dentists call it? Diastema? "Diner Zen, Sam. Hey, your girlfriend's here again." She tilted her head to a back booth where Wendy sat watching us. "Watch out; people are starting to talk."

"Good. I could use the publicity."

She nodded. "Right." She handed me one of the cups from the tray. "Don't let your fingers get too close to her teeth."

"Meow."

"Oh that's cruel. I told you my cat died." She set down the pot and brushed that stray strand of hair behind her ear.

"And now you're channeling him?"

She bounced a rolled up counter rag off my forehead, laughing. "Beat it. Unlike you I got a job to do here."

Wendy sat in the booth with a cup of tea, the tag dangling over the side like a hero in some cliffhanger movie. "She really wants you, Sam."

"Oh, you read minds too?"

"No, just body language. I've spent years of my life interviewing people who don't want to tell me what I need to know."

"And what's my body saying?"

"Feed me." She tilted her head back and looked at my shirt logo from the bottom of her eyes. "Fur Peace Ranch—is that a high end brothel?"

"Remember Jorma Kaukonen from Jefferson Airplane?"

"And Hot Tuna? Yeah, I know who you mean."

"The Fur Peace Ranch is his guitar camp. I went there for a seminar once. I took Jorma's advanced level class on fingerstyle blues."

"Sounds like fun. Was it worthwhile?"

"Oh, yeah. I learned a lot about playing guitar, but the most important lesson you learn there is that there's a cartload of really good guitar players out there and none of them has a monopoly on talent."

Wendy thought that over for a minute and changed tack. "Did you find Barton's phony act the other day as offensive as I did?"

I nodded. "It was absolutely calculated to jerk tears. He's desperate to salvage his career because he's afraid he can't survive without Eddie's hand in the songwriting." I snorted. "Encourage and foster young songwriters, my ass. What a crock. Find out who's talented and naïve and rip them off, more like it."

"I think you're right. He's milking the media for all he can get. 'Carry On' will keep him in the public eye—or ear—for a long time, and every time some kid gets the scholarship, his picture will be all over the newspapers and TV. It's the gift that keeps on giving."

"And as for money, he won't get any cash from that song, but it'll be on a CD and he'll get royalties from the other eight or ten. Bastard. I tuned in when the commercials were running. Did he say much before then? "

"It was all fluff, and in every sentence with Eddie's name he attached at least one 'we.' I wish I was on Donna Fields' stool today instead of that fawning hairdo. I wonder how Danny Barton would fare with a real reporter."

"I'd pay money to see that interview. Why don't you call him?"

Wendy played with her pen. "Who says I didn't?"

"And he wouldn't talk, right?"

"He wouldn't even acknowledge the calls."

"Doesn't know what he's missing. So that's why you're still talking to me, huh?"

One corner of her mouth turned up in a smile. "No, Sam, you're interesting in your own right."

She ordered a Western omelet and I ordered ham and eggs. Jenny took our order, and as she walked away, she turned and behind Wendy's back took a big air bite.

Wendy fished the teabag out of her mug with a spoon and wrapped the string around it. She squeezed the bag until it bled almost white.

Time to change the subject. I pointed to her teabag. "There's a metaphor."

"What? I like strong tea."

"I was thinking about squeezing people, the way you and Kearny do. Which one of you's the spoon?" I saw something angry flicker in her eyes. I grinned. "Just messin' with you."

She set down the spoon and put both hands flat on the table. "Get this straight, Sam, I get some tips from Mike, and when I get something on a case that will help him nail some SOB, I give it to him, but I'm not his silent partner." Her lips pressed together. Either she was a terrific actress, or I'd hit a nerve. Mike, eh?

I resisted the urge to say, "Calm down." Instead, I said, "Good to know. Because I know a few things he doesn't yet, and I intend to make sure that this fish ain't the one that gets away. Kearny thinks Eddie's murder and Lottie's are in the same box. I agree."

She stirred her tea idly. The gears were turning. "And is this the moment when the brilliant amateur detective reveals the identity of the killer to the clueless reporter?"

"No, but I need some help. I can handle a computer okay with music, but not much else. How are you with digital images?"

At that moment, Jenny brought our order. She fussed just a little too long at the booth, and Wendy radiated impatience like a Franklin stove. Jenny said pointedly to me, "Can I get you anything else?"

"We're good, thank you." Wendy's tone was sub-zero.

Jenny smiled at her and said sweetly, "I'll check with you later."

Ignoring her, Wendy said, "Where were we?"

"I have some pictures that I need to see up close, and maybe enhanced, like you see in cop shows. Can you do that without blowing the whistle to Kearny? You might get the story of the year."

"Now who's the spoon? " She gave it a minute while she sipped her tea, her eyes shifting from one side to the other, as if the pros and cons were on opposite ends of the table. Finally she gave me the head-on look again and said, "I can do that. I have the latest version of Photoshop on my laptop, but no promises on the cops." She grinned a wicked one. "That is, 'til after I file my story."

Halfway through breakfast, my cell phone rang. It was Joe Mancini. "Excuse me; it's my agent." Her eyebrows raised. "Yes, I have an agent. Yeah, Joe."

"Hey, Sam, I have good news! I booked you for a showcase party this week."

"Short notice; somebody cancel?"

"Nope, they asked for you."

Showcase parties are a recent development in mid-range pop music. A host (often an enamored fan) provides a location, usually a living room, and refreshments. The artist plays a private show for a limited number of guests, rarely more than twenty. Unlike an ordinary party, the guests at a showcase pay fifty to a hundred dollars apiece for the privilege of an up-close, intimate experience.

Like so many fads, this one offers bragging rights: exclusivity, hearing songs that haven't hit the air yet, and personal schmoozing with the performer. My benefit aside from a good paycheck is an opportunity to try out new material and gauge response much more easily than I could with a large crowd; I see faces, body language, and attitude changes I couldn't see from a stage. Also, I sell a pile of my CDs and occasionally get laid.

I'd played a few of these in the last year, most of them a moderate distance from home. Like Will Rogers' definition of an expert, an entertaining performer is someone who lives more than fifty miles away, but this party was local in tony Bell Heights.

"Acoustic okay?"

"Up to you." Joe gave me the details and signed off.

"Big gig?"

"Big enough; a showcase party in town."

She nodded. "I've heard of them. Never been to one."

"Invitation only."

"So am I invited?"

"Sure. You can be my roadie. Better yet, I'll tell Joe you're doing a feature on me. He'll make it work. Actually the guests may get off on it, thinking they might make the papers. An extra added attraction."

"What's the deal with going acoustic?"

"I'd rather play showcases with an unamplified guitar and natural voice. Give 'em the straight stuff; otherwise I might as well just pop a CD in the karaoke machine. Remember MTV's *Unplugged* show?" She nodded.

While it lasted, I really liked MTV's *Unplugged*. Rock stars and even Tony Bennett did their hits live with nothing but acoustic instruments. *Unplugged* separated real musicians from fakers, and I was surprised, for example, to see Kiss — sans makeup — pull it off with real flair.

"I saw Jackson Browne do a live acoustic show by himself last year. I was impressed. I can't wait to see how you do it." She dabbed the corners of her mouth with a napkin. "So, let's get digital. Your place or mine?"

In Dora's parking lot, Wendy pulled out her keys and said, "I'll follow you, and then you won't have to bring me back here when we're done." Clever girl, and cautious; leave an escape hatch. She's been around.

"Okay. That's my ride over there."

She gaped at my red Dodge Caravan. "You drive a soccer mom car?"

"Greatest gift the automotive industry ever gave the musician. Fold down the back seat and you can haul five people and equipment. Take out the middle seats and you can haul a whole band's worth of gear. This is my third Caravan since they started making them in the 80s. I just leave my big stuff in the back all the time. It makes for less loading and unloading. "

She shook her head in disbelief. "I'd believe a flowered Volkswagen microbus. Or even a retired police cruiser like the Blues Brothers, but a Caravan?" She thumbed her key fob and lights flashed on a grey Acura Legend three spaces over.

"At least one of us rides in style. Follow me; it's not far."

15

We lucked out. There were two spaces on the street near my building. In the elevator a different Bible tract was lying on the floor: *God Loves You.* The tract was punched through by a spiked heel.

Wendy laughed when she walked into my apartment. "Rita Rudner says that single men live 'like bears with furniture.' I guess you're the exception, or do you pay a maid?"

I took her jacket and hung it on the coat tree. "Not all musicians live in squalor; only most of them. You oughta see Cotton Breakiron's crib. It's like living in wreckage."

"I'll pass," she said, crossing the room to my bookshelves. "Definitely a man-cave, though. No feminine touches here."

"I'm, shall we say, between relationships, like for about the last five years."

She laughed, running a finger over the spines of a row of books. "This sure isn't Gatsby's library, either. Did you abuse all of these yourself, or did you buy them beat up?"

"Read 'em all a dozen times each; the curse of the English major."

"Yeah. I heard you taught college courses." She picked up a tattered paperback lying alone on top of a bookcase. "Robert Frost. I pegged you as a Wallace Stevens fan, or maybe Hart Crane."

"The bottom of the sea is cruel," I intoned in my best professor voice. "I like all three. But as a songwriter, I appreciate Frost's handling of rhyming metered verse. I learned a lot from reading him."

She nodded, putting the book back on the shelf. "I never had time to read as much poetry as I'd like. Journalism is a harsh—I can't say mistress—mister? I read mostly non-fiction now; biographies are more interesting to me." She moved to the instrument wall. "Do you have names for all your guitars?"

"No, why do you ask?"

"B. B. King has Lucille, Eric Clapton has Brown Betty. Why do guys always name their guitars after women?"

I shrugged. "The same reason they call ships 'she,' I guess. Freud says 'sometimes a cigar is just a cigar,' but at the same time Lacan says that guitars are like swords or guns or baseball bats; they're all phallic extensions."

"Frost, Freud, Lacan—you're full of surprises, Sam." Then she pursed her lips in disgust. "That Lacan crack puts a whole new slant on Danny Barton hugging his guitar like he was in love with it. I thought it was just part of the show. Yuck."

"Worked for Donna Fields, didn't it?"

She rolled her eyes and reached for her bag. "Speaking of Freud, where do I plug in?"

Wendy sat at my desk and bulldozed my clutter out of the way with her laptop as she flipped it open. I gave her Lottie's CD and she booted up. "Want coffee? Tea? A beer?"

She shook her head, her eyes never leaving the computer. "Maybe later." I fetched a kitchen chair to sit beside her so that I could see the screen.

In a minute, her startup was running and she was pulling up the menu.

My computer boots up to a frame from Fritz Lang's *Metropolis*, the mountainous Moloch-machine that personifies capitalism devouring the proletariat. There but for fortune. I wasn't surprised that her laptop showed the stock Windows desktop; all business, no whimsy. "What do you need enhanced?"

"Lottie Williams took the pictures on this disk the day Eddie was killed." That got her attention. She turned and gave me a questioning look. "Pull up the directory and scroll through the pictures. I'll tell you when to stop."

She clicked on the first file and the picture flashed onto the screen. "I'll just click through them." She stopped at a close up, studying it. "He looks pretty good for thirty-nine. Did he have a face lift?"

"Don't know."

"He has the classic strong chin, blue eyes, and that thick head of blonde hair. That and his casual air of self-confidence; he doesn't have to try and he knows it. I can see why women would love him and men would hate him. This is nice work, by the way. Lottie had a good eye for composition. With a little editing, this would pass muster with any major magazine." When the first shot of Eddie leaning on the desk appeared, I said, "Stop."

"O-ka-a-ay," her voice trailed off and her brow wrinkled as she studied the photo. "What am I seeing, or maybe the big question is, what are you seeing?"

I pointed to Eddie's right hand. "Can you zoom in on that hand, the one with the cigarette?"

She nodded and thumbed the touchpad. In a few seconds, Eddie's right hand filled the screen. "There: the ring. Can you find the date and time for this picture?"

She nodded. "What about the ring?" She clicked back to the directory and right clicked the file. The Properties menu read October 2nd at 4:32 P.M.

"What did the coroner estimate as time of death?"

"For Eddie? Between seven and midnight."

"There was no ring on Eddie's hand when he came to the morgue, but he's wearing it here."

Wendy said hesitantly, "Does Kearny know this?"

"We talked about it the day I decked him. But he doesn't know about this picture."

"Are we withholding evidence?"

"Of what? I told him Eddie never took off the ring. He told me it was missing when they brought him to the morgue. This picture just confirms what he already knows."

She nodded again, a little less worried this time. "Is there anything else?"

"Yeah. Can you move over to the desk behind him?"

She shifted the picture to center the desk clutter on the screen. I pointed. "Zoom in there, the desk. Can you make that more detailed?"

"I'll try some of the filters." She clicked back and forth between menus and the detail became more and less distinct as she tried different applications. "That's about as good as it'll get. Zoom in again?"

"Yeah." I looked carefully at the screen. "Dammit. I thought I could read what was on the papers on his desk if you turned the picture upside down. It's too fuzzy."

"I can't zoom much more or it'll pixellate into squares."

"Can we try a few of the others?"

It was the same story. "Oh, hell. I thought I might find a clue. Sorry, I guess I wasted your time."

"Not at all. Could I copy this picture for future reference?"

"I don't know how that would fly legally, considering it's Lottie's pic, and she can't give consent. How about I give you my word that you'll have first crack at it once I know it's kosher?"

"Fair enough. Just don't peddle it elsewhere."

"Our little secret."

"For now." She stood up and pushed back her chair. "How about that beer?"

"One minute." I reached down and pushed the eject button on her disc drive. I took out the disk and put it back in its case. I smiled; she smiled. Busted.

When I came back from the kitchen, I found Wendy studying the group of old band photos hanging near the TV set. "So many bands; where's your family?"

"Both my parents are gone. No brothers, no sisters. I have some cousins in Michigan, but they're the closest relatives I've got. I guess the music community is my extended family now."

The next hour passed in pleasant conversation. In her own way, Wendy was charming when she wasn't in probe mode and I was more relaxed with her, less wary that anything I said would show up in print. She knew a lot about a lot that I didn't, and vice versa, not an intellectual dog and pony show, but we were both preening a little. It was fun to talk with someone with more depth than a shot glass.

"So tell me about songwriting."

"Like you said before, it's mostly 'small money.' I write the songs and record demos of them, and Joe shops them around. Every once in a while somebody likes one and it ends up on an LP. Sometimes I get up front money, sometimes royalties. Not enough to live on by itself, but it's one piece of the pie.

"The good old days are gone when you could land your song on the B-side of somebody's single and if the A-side sold a million copies, so did yours. Napster and iTunes fragmented the market, for good or ill, and the whole business changed. A handful of people make the really big bucks; that hasn't changed, and for the rest of us, it's still a dogfight. Most of my cash still comes from playing one-nighters, but that's changed too."

"How so?"

"Before, people went to a club or a bar to see an artist perform. The new generation goes not to see but to be seen at whatever place is currently trendy. DJs, karaoke, free jukebox, live band; it's all Muzak for the young posers. These days it's all a backdrop for selfies."

"And you work strictly solo?"

"Most of the time."

"Does that mean you don't play well with others?" Her eyes crinkled at the corners. She was waiting to see if I caught the pun.

I laughed. "That means I got tired of playing with guys who equate being loud with being good, haul two truckloads of equipment around, take two hours to set up and an hour to tear down and come back to town as the sun comes up. I went from all that to a guitar, a microphone and a stool. I rarely play later than midnight or drive more than half an hour to a gig, and I make the same money."

"You don't play in bands at all now?"

"Sometimes I fill in when somebody needs a guitarist or a bass player, but usually I fly solo."

She looked over to the guitars. "Think you could ever write a hit song about me?"

"Probably not. What rhymes with Wendy?"

"Trendy." She was quick.

Rhyming 'reporter' would be a stretch too." I thought for a minute and sang to the tune of "Celito Lindo":

There once was a gal name of Wendy
Undeniably hip and quite trendy
And a stellar reporter but nobody'd court her
Because her morals weren't bendy.

She laughed and tilted the neck of her bottle at me. "You're really loopy, you know that?"

"I was the undisputed limerick champion of Phi Kappa Sigma in college."

"You're kidding. I can't see you as a frat boy."

"Like you said, I'm full of surprises. How about you? Were you Suzie Sorority?"

She shook her head. "No time."

"Too busy learning to change the world, huh?"

She gave me a quizzical look. "Change the world?"

"A couple of years ago I read about a survey of Columbia Journalism majors. Eighty percent of them said they wanted to be journalists so they could 'change the world' or something like that." I put on my professor voice. "Not report the news in an unbiased fashion, not seek out and present the unvarnished truth. Change the world; the reporter as activist. Is that you?"

Wendy shook her head. "Nope. I kinda like the world the way it is. Keeps me employed writing about it."

"So tell me about being a newshound."

"Hunter Thompson nailed it in *The Curse of Llono*. Ever read that one?" I shook my head. "Thompson said that the reason reporters put up with the long hours, low pay and all the other crap that comes with the job is they get to pursue whatever interests them and someone else picks up the tab. More truth in that than you can imagine."

"But why crime reporting? Is it a personal obsession or something to prove?"

She thought about that one for a minute. "Maybe when I started, but now it's a way of life. I don't have to prove anything to anybody anymore. I hold my own."

Type two ego, I thought. I raised my beer to her. "Here's to next year's Pulitzer."

She clinked her bottle on mine. "Or this year's—and a Grammy."

Feet on the coffee table, we watched my DVD of Danny's *Jumpstart* performance. "The title, 'Carry On,' wasn't that the name of a Kansas song way back?"

"Yeah, and one by a group of emo rockers called Fun, and one by a metal band, Avenged Sevenfold, and one by a rapper called Kid Ink. You can't copyright a title. I could write a song and call it 'When I'm Sixty-Four,' and Paul McCartney couldn't sue me, even if he needed the money."

"The title's a great pun."

"How so?"

"'Carry On,' carrion. He's exploiting Eddie's death like a crow pecking at road kill."

How did I miss that one? She was even sharper than I thought.

We ran the clip a few more times. Wendy impressed me with the subtle nuances she spotted in Danny, Donna, and Trey's behavior. "Donna Fields is too easy. See how she reaches behind her head, fixing her hair? She's primping. She knows better than to do that on camera, but she can't help herself; it's subconscious. She's exposing her wrists to Danny; it's a courting gesture.

"And Trey is more interested in her than he is in his guest," she said. "Look at his feet. The toes are pointed past him at her; dead giveaway. And when he speaks to Barton, he's flashing that smile but his shoulders are rigid. Standard Alpha male behavior: posturing for a rival."

"How about Danny? Where are his toes pointing?"

"Probably at a mirror." She aimed the remote at the DVR and reversed the video, stopping on a close shot of Danny's face. "I can't see his eyes as well as I'd like behind those glasses, but he's rubbing his lip while he's talking, covering his mouth. He isn't comfortable with what he's saying. I'd say he's full of shit."

Wendy turned down a second beer and left soon after that. Errands to run, she said. I shut the door and sank onto the sofa, playing "Carry On" one more time. I may have wasted Wendy's time with the pictures, but I didn't waste mine. Kearny didn't show her the crime scene photos or she would have said I could read the paperwork on the desk from them. Or as devious as Wendy was, she could be sandbagging me. And if she didn't mention Lottie's photos of Eddie to Kearny, she'd be sandbagging him. The whole business gave me a headache.

I couldn't read the fine print from the picture, but the enhanced image of Eddie's desk showed not, two, but three copyright forms with filled in blanks on the top one. I decided Wendy was right. Danny was full of shit.

16

I always hated funerals, and memorial services run a close second. If you weren't there for the dead guy when he was alive, it seems a phony gesture to show up after the fact, but I set aside my prejudices for Eddie. He'd been dead for eight days, and the coroner finally released the body.

The service was held in the chapel of Kyle's Funeral Home. If Eddie set foot in a church any time past the age of parental control, it would be news to anybody who knew him, and it didn't seem right to drag him into one when he was too dead to protest. Eddie didn't believe in God, the Devil, white light, or an afterlife and would tell anyone who'd listen to him. I can only assume he meant it.

There were more empty seats than filled ones when I came in. I saw some other people I recognized down front, musicians, roadies, recording engineers and a couple of suits from Sunsong. It would have been a good opportunity to network if it wouldn't have looked so ghoulish. I took a seat two rows from the back.

Eddie's parents were both dead, killed in a plane crash three weeks after his father retired from the steel mill. His body would be shipped home to be buried beside them. Eddie had a brother in the Air Force and a sister in Florida, but neither made the service. I wondered whether they'd show up when his will was read. Eddie's girlfriend was conspicuously absent too. That left Danny, who stood by the casket solemnly shaking hands with the sympathetic. I wondered who would stand by his casket. I'd volunteer just to make sure he stayed in it.

Eddie's casket was open. He had the same blank look on his face as I'd seen in the crime scene photos. He was dressed in a black suit, white shirt and red tie. His hands were folded over the coffin blanket, his ring hand strategically hidden by the other. Kearny's request? Lottie should have been there, snapping Eddie's last appearance. There were no cameras allowed in the room, but I suspected that clandestine cell phone snaps and videos would show up in the tabloids if not on the evening news courtesy of the new paparazzi.

Gin Sing's album *Top Shelf* played in the background. I can't say softly, but low enough that the music allowed conversation. It hasn't happened yet, but I dread the day I listen to "Cold Fire" in an elevator all the way to the lobby or in the grocery section of Wal-Mart.

Danny looked even older than he did on *Jumpstart* but not as much as I do. His face was still angular, but starting to sag at the corners of the mouth. He was wearing his glasses. Apparently they'd become a fixture on his face. I was surprised that vanity didn't push him to wear contact lenses instead, but maybe all the smoke around him made them impractical.

Danny's suit would pay for five of the one I wore, but that didn't bother me. Like the TV cable, why pay a grand for a suit I hardly ever wore when I could pay two hundred and wear it just as seldom. Perspective is a great substitute for money.

Wendy came in, scanned the room, and sat beside me. "What have I missed?"

I turned to her and gave her a half smile. "Not a thing. The show's about to start. Get out your notebook." She ignored me. Over her shoulder, I saw Kearny leaning against the wall near the door; tan suit today. He studiously ignored me too. I felt like waving to him like we used to do to the undercover narcs when I was in college, but I thought better of it. No sense annoying him. Cotton came in soon after and plopped down on my other side.

"Wendy Conn, meet Cotton Breakiron." Their pleasantries were cut short when Burton Kyle stepped up to the podium beside Eddie's casket and tapped lightly on the microphone.

Mortuary colleges must teach a course called "Undertaker's Persona" that invests the student with that weird mix of sympathy, gravity, and deference that comforts the bereaved but on the street makes the undertaker seem like Norman Bates. It's all a matter of context; like Lon Chaney once said, "a clown isn't funny in the moonlight." Kyle was anything but funny; in fact he was anything but anything. In a neutral grey suit with a neutral white shirt and a neutral navy blue necktie, he was as innocuous a person as he could be; nothing to excite, distract or offend. I didn't expect him to wear a red tie with a palm tree and a fringed hula dancer, but there was a complete absence of personality in his clothes. If he stood still too long he'd fade into the wallpaper like a chameleon.

Kyle raised his hands and said in a quiet voice that still cut through the chatter, "Friends . . ."

"Romans and countrymen," I muttered. Why do they always use that word? Wendy elbowed me in the ribs. "Sh!" she hissed.

"Today we meet to remember the life of Edmund Shay." Edmund? Kyle probably read that on the death certificate. Eddie hated his formal name and nobody but his grandmother had called him that since he hit puberty. I half expected him to reach out of his casket and swat Kyle across the back of his head. Kyle's aesthetic awareness was limited to arranging flowers and sculpting replacement noses from mortician's wax. He didn't know Eddie from Tiny Tim.

Kyle went on, "His band mate and long-time friend Daniel Barton will now deliver the eulogy and afterward, if any among you wish to share a remembrance of Edmund..."

"Eddie, dude," a voice piped up from one of the long-hairs near the front. It was Gin Sing's current bass player Joe Craig. "He called himself Eddie."

"That's right, man," Zip Morris, the drummer chimed in.

Kyle turned his head toward Craig and Zip and gave them the same indulgent smile you might give a precocious eight-year-old. "If any of you wishes to share a remembrance of . . ." he hesitated, turning his head to the side thoughtfully, "Eddie," Kyle spoke the name as if he'd discovered a new word, "you may do so following the eulogy."

Danny stepped behind the little podium where he shuffled some papers. At least he was smart enough to not risk spontaneity. "We're all here to celebrate a life; a life full of creativity, a life full of music, and a life full of love." Tell that to all the broken hearts he left in his wake, I thought.

"I knew Eddie," Danny went on. "Probably better than anyone in this room, and I know Eddie wouldn't want us to cry, he'd want us to smile over all the good music and good times he shared with us. I know he'd want us to laugh at the great cosmic joke life is. He'd want us to spit in Death's eye and raise one more glass to his memory."

I nudged Wendy. "Gonna write that one down?"

Her mouth twisted into an irritated sneer. "Not necessary. Some things are so awful they're unforgettable."

Danny was a pretty good lyricist, good enough to fill twelve Gin Sing CDs, and his eulogy had a few poetic touches, but he followed the egotist's cardinal rule: "I" before" he" except after "we." Listening to Danny, you could believe that Eddie never did anything in his life without Danny welded to his hip. After five minutes of it, I tuned out and Danny droned on. When he stopped, Kyle came forward. "Would anyone else wish to share some remembrance of the departed?"

A few musicians and fans stepped up and stumbled through praises punctuated with "y'know," "like," and "man." When they finished, Kyle asked, "Are there any others who would care to say a few words?"

Danny stood and waved a hand in my general direction. "We have an original Gin Sing member with us, Sam Dunne, who knew Eddie as well as any of us did. Do you want to say something, Sam?"

That took me by surprise. Everyone turned to look at me. I stared Danny down, gave a three count and slowly shook my head. "No thanks. I think you got it covered."

Danny didn't move for a second, but I saw the corners of his mouth turn upward just a little, as if he'd just received an epiphany. He took off his glasses and I could see his eyes narrow, see through them to the gears turning inside that twisted head of his. He was weighing things, scheming, and that couldn't be good.

Someone I hadn't noticed earlier stood up and moved beside the coffin. She stood at Eddie's head while Danny moved to his feet.

It was Alana Jeffries, lead singer for Cold Shot, in a long black dress and a veil. Without her onstage tramp chic wardrobe, she looked almost demure as she began to sing an old Gin Sing hit *a capella*. She had a strong alto voice that pierced every heart in the place with its sweet power. "We

"Do you want to say something, Sam?"

lived and we loved together long enough for our hearts to grow strong, but now you're gone I find that I have lived a day too long." She slowed the pop rock tempo of the song and put a bluesy lilt to her delivery. "All that life has left for me is to sing a dead man's melody." She repeated the tag and held the word "sing" in a long, impossibly high vibrato note and ran the last word from her highest range to her lowest like a skier slaloming down a black diamond mountain. The song ended to a stunned silence. I didn't catch it, but Cotton did. He whispered, "I think she passed the audition. The guys from Sunsong just started breathing again."

Then Kyle stepped forward and said, "And that concludes the service."

No shit. How could anybody follow that number?

"See you, Sam. Deadline." Wendy scurried off, pausing to say something in Kearny's ear before she went out the door.

Cotton has a gift for saying things with a straight face that make me fall on the floor laughing, and then he stands wide-eyed and innocent, looking at me as if I'm having a seizure. As the mourners drifted toward the back of the room, he said, "What an impressive eulogy," then *sotto voce*, he ambushed me. "That be some world class horseshit." I laughed out loud before I could catch myself, earning dirty looks from some of the departing. No comment from the departed.

Kearny worked his way over to me as Cotton and I stood up. He dispensed with formality. "Not too many people here."

"Don't be so disappointed. You only need one if it's the right one. See anybody you like?" I jibed. My joke earned me a flat stare from Kearny. "No, nobody I like," he said in a humorless voice, emphasis on "nobody."

Kyle stopped in passing to say hello to Kearny. "You know everybody, don't you?" I said.

Kearny gave me the half-eye look. "No, mostly just bad guys—and musicians. Burton Kyle's a deputy coroner. You could say we do a lot of business together." He turned to Cotton. "And you're Cotton Breakiron."

"I know you?"

I broke in, "This is Detective Kearny from homicide."

"Oh, yeah!" Cotton broke out his most disingenuous smile. "I see you on TV, every time somebody get killed."

"And I see you blowin' tenor at The Regent every time I can afford the two drink minimum."

Cotton switched from hip hop hooligan to PBS announcer: "Always happy to meet an aficionado, officer." Cotton's segues could give you whiplash.

Kearny turned back to me and flicked out his trigger finger in my direction like a switchblade knife. "Talk to you later." He gave Cotton a nod and headed for the door. Talk to me later. I wondered whether that was something I should worry about.

Cotton's smile snapped off like rubber band. "Man, I hate cops, especially cops who know my name."

"So next time you're mugged, call a saxophonist." I pronounced it the way Phillis Diller did: *sax-off-o-nist.*

"Call me some cracker git-tar player, more the like. Let you get *your* honky ass shot off." We both laughed at that one, and Cotton said, "Outta here, Sam. Duty calls."

"Or is that 'booty'?" He rolled his eyes, pasted on a dreamy smile, and stalked off leaving me alone.

The Gin Sing entourage moved to the Rainbow, a bar on 23rd, to drink an early lunch. Zip invited me along, but I passed on it. I was afraid that if I stood too close to Danny my head would explode. I went instead to Harrigan's and sat alone at a dark corner of the bar with a sandwich and a beer. The noon news showed clips of the mourners coming out of Kyle's with Danny leading the pack. The sound was off, so I didn't hear what Danny told the reporter, but I could guess. I figured he was giving a condensed version of his eulogy. I'd be surprised if he didn't have copies of it printed up to pass out to the press.

17

Eddie's memorial service was on Monday, Lottie's funeral was the next day. Her family and a few co-workers from the hospital gathered at the Saint Sebastian Catholic Church on 28th Street for the standard Christian Mass of Burial. There was no viewing. The rock'n'roll contingent was absent, maybe because her family was a little embarrassed at the way she spent her free time and didn't extend the invitation. Or maybe they kept it quiet because they didn't want the press ambushing them from behind the sacristy. I found out about the funeral by accident, running into Mae Stern, an ER nurse, the night before. I debated calling Wendy but decided I should do this one alone.

I was raised a Methodist, for all the good it did me, and a few people gave me stern looks when I didn't genuflect in the aisle or kneel when they did. We can't all be Catholics. After the Mass, I followed the procession to the church cemetery on Polish Hill. It was raining, a cold, misty drizzle that made me turn up my collar. I thought of T-Bone Walker: "They call it stormy Monday, but Tuesday's just as bad." No hope for a brighter tomorrow in that song.

The priest swung his censer, said his prayers, and headed for the limo. I stepped forward and reached into my coat, pulled out a rose and laid it on the coffin. "Goodbye, Lottie," I whispered. As I stepped back, a short woman with Lottie's build and Lottie's eyes left the knot of family and came over. Raindrops mixed with the tears on her cheeks. She held out a hand to me. "I'm Jean Williams. I'm Lottie's mother."

I took her hand; it felt as cold as mine. "I'm very sorry for your loss, ma'am. I can't imagine what this must have done to all of you."

"Thank you." A pause. "You're Sam Dunne." I nodded. "I recognized you from some of Lottie's pictures. She always said good things about you. Thank you for coming. She'd be glad to know you were here." At a loss for meaningful words, I nodded again, and she went back to her family.

I expected to see Kearny crouched behind one of the tombstones like a graveyard ghoul, watching for the killer at the funeral like some cheap 40s gangster movie, but I was disappointed. Priorities. Just like the best seat on an airplane or the best table in a restaurant, I guess the celebrity gets the best murder investigation too. I promised Lottie and promised myself that this one wouldn't end up in a cold case file.

18

Joe landed me a really plum gig that Wednesday night, the Avalanche lounge at Snowcrest, a ski resort twenty miles out of town. Snow wasn't coming any day soon, but the place ran year-round for the restaurant, banquet and convention business. I had played there for years, then management changed. The first thing new managers do in a place like that is pitch the Rolodex and hire their friends. Snowcrest was no exception, but somehow, Joe got me the gig. I was hoping it would lead to more of the same.

The Avalanche is a big flashy room that swallows an off-season crowd, maybe fifty people that night. A wall of windows shows off the lighted ski slopes in the winter and reflects the bar light when the slopes are dark.

As a result, the place looks twice as cavernous as it is. Like too many bars these days, the Avalanche has a dozen or more big-screen TV sets flashing around the room, each one tuned to a different sports event. I long for the days when people came to a club or a bar to listen to live music, not use it for background while they watched NFL highlights and got drunk. The stage is a big one, built and outfitted to accommodate a full-sized band, and it dwarfed me like the room did the crowd.

The Avalanche offers one exceptional feature, a first-rate PA system complete with Mark Smith, the house sound man. I plugged my guitar into my amp and my amp into the system. Mark did the rest, and it always sounded good. Besides, at my age, I've learned that those hundred pound speaker cabinets are never going to get any lighter. The downside, if there was one, was the nine-to-one clock on the job. Four hours can drag on forever with a slow crowd. I looked out at the empty tables and recalled something Robert Frost said: "Hell is a half empty auditorium." Then I remembered something Joe Mancini always said: "They're payin', you're playin'."

I couldn't see faces very well with the stage lights head-on, but I could see that most of the crowd was in the back section of the room. They could hear me, but I was incidental to their evening. I made up my mind a long time ago that large crowd or small, interested or not, I come to play, and give a good show for five people or five hundred. That's as much pragmatism as it is professionalism; if I play a lousy show one week, I won't be back to do a good one the next.

The first few songs, I feel out the crowd, seeing what they like and getting an idea of how to work them the rest of the gig. Self-help books teach that your first fifteen seconds of contact are worth your next fifteen minutes. The music business version of that rule of thumb is your first four songs are worth your next four hours.

I opened with an old standby, John Hiatt's "I'm a Real Man" and followed with my song "Hourglass." I rounded out the foursome with Steve Acho's off-beat arrangement of "Hey Soul Sister" and Gary Moore's haunting "Still Got the Blues For You." Like the wedding rhyme says, "something old, something new, something borrowed, something blue." I got some scattered applause and nobody yelled for "Free Bird," so I figured I was okay.

Unlike a quiet place like Casey's, this room demanded a meatier rhythm guitar and a faster tempo. People here would be toe tappers, and the music had to keep that vibe going. I played two hours straight then took a break, heading for the bar for a beer, schmoozing with the crowd on the way. Mark put on one of my CDs to fill the void. Halfway to the bar I spotted Danny Barton at a table flanked by a good looking brunette and a guy my age. Danny waved me over and I threaded my way through the tables.

"Sam, good to see you; you haven't lost your touch. Still sound great." Danny stood and gestured to an empty chair then to his friends. "Sit down. Say hello to Marie and Bob." I nodded to both and sat. Danny looked a little less chunky than he had on TV; his jacket seemed to hang a little bit looser. Not quite a scarecrow, but headed in that direction. He looked tired, a little bit haggard. Eddie's murder was taking a toll on all of us. His hair was pulled back into a ponytail, and the bar lights flickered on a diamond stud in his ear.

Danny went on, "Sam was the third eye of Gin Sing in the old days. Wrote 'Cold Fire,' you know?"

Bob nodded. "Great song." Bob had the artificial, sleek look people get from too much paid attention. His suit, his haircut, his suntan and his Caz glasses said money but not wealth. I had him pegged as upper management, maybe from Sunsong. Marie was late twenties trying for early and almost succeeding with a red dress that showed a lot of cleavage. Her model-perfect set of teeth flashed in a practiced smile.

"Haven't seen you in a while, Sam," Danny said over the music.

"Didn't know you were looking." A waitress appeared and I ordered a Heineken. Danny ordered a fresh Tanqueray and tonic and daiquiris for Bob and Marie. "Saw you on *Jumpstart*."

"He nodded. That was some shit with Eddie, wasn't it?" He took a pull at his drink. "Sure gonna miss him."

Bob cut in, "You have a nice style, Sam, especially the interplay between your vocals and the guitar. Danny speaks very highly of you and I can see why."

I nodded. "Thanks. You play guitar for thirty-odd years, you pick up a few tricks."

He smiled at my self-deprecating humor. "And you work the crowd well. This isn't the easiest room on the planet."

"Sam's an old hand at it all. "Danny tipped his glass at me. "And he writes good stuff too. That's his CD playing."

Bob listened for a moment and nodded. "I'm impressed."

The drinks arrived. A little more small talk and then Danny did what I'd expected; he turned to Bob and said, "Could you excuse us for few minutes?" Bob nodded. "Come on, Marie, I'll show you the new aquarium." She pouted but stood.

"That's okay," I said. "No need for you to leave. I'm going back on in a minute anyway. Don't want to alienate the management."

"You won't," said Bob. "Take as long as you like. I run Snowcrest." He and Marie walked away, drinks in hand, leaving me with Danny. I took a long pull of the Heineken and set the bottle on the table, rolling it between my fingers. "Do we call this an 'arranged meeting?' Did you get me this gig?"

He smiled, showing a few teeth. "We could call it that; as for the gig, Bob's a friend. I wanted him to hear you. But I'd rather think of tonight as catching up and mending fences." He was wearing the same tinted glasses he wore on TV and the colored glare from the bar hid his eyes. "I've always felt really bad about kicking you out, Sam, but Sunsong insisted. I did get them to agree to put 'Cold Fire' and 'Downhill Slide' on the LP so you'd get some royalties, but I always thought you got a raw deal."

We both knew that was complete bullshit. When I didn't respond, he filled the uncomfortable silence. "You know Eddie wrote the tunes, and he was damned good. I can't do it nearly as well as he did, but from what I've heard tonight from you..." Danny gestured to acknowledge "Top Thirteen" playing over the PA system. "I think you can fill his shoes." Again, I kept my mouth shut. I figured if I didn't fuel the conversation, he'd run out of small talk and get to the point. "I thought maybe we could work together again."

"Like you said, it's been a long time. Neither of us is the same as we were."

"You're right, Sam. We're not the same; we're better. In every way."

"I have the feeling that we wouldn't be having this conversation if Eddie were still alive."

He lowered his eyebrows and pursed his lips. I got the impression he rehearsed his faces in front of a mirror. "Losing Eddie is a real blow. We were working up the last LP of our contract with Sunsong, and we weren't sure what would happen next. Now I really don't know"

"Word is that Eddie wanted out. True?"

"That's crap; has been every time that story made the rounds. But now it's happened anyway." He took a hit from his drink and took a deep breath. "And I have an LP to finish and I need three more songs."

"Counting 'Carry On'?'"

"Yeah, counting 'Carry On'."

"I have some new ones nobody's heard yet. You could fill out the CD with them."

He pulled at his lower lip. "Well, I thought we could work together, kinda keep the Gin Sing brand alive. I wasn't thinking in terms of 'me'; I was thinking in terms of 'we.'"

The greedy bastard wanted a piece of every cut on the LP; "we" to do the work, "he" to grab the money.

I took a long pull out of my bottle and gave him a hard stare. "Full credit, full cut?" He hesitated and finally nodded. "We could probably work that out."

"And you have Sunsong's authority to make that offer?"

"They thought it had possibilities." He tried to smile again but it stuck halfway. This wasn't going the easy way he thought it would.

I've learned that people never change; they just show sides of themselves you haven't seen before. Danny Barton was approaching me one-on-one, so I was already what the label wanted; he was hustling to line things up to his advantage before they talked to me. Since we were horse trading, I asked for the Universe. "And do I play on the LP?"

Again the hesitation. "That's not my call." For the first time that night, he looked away.

"Then maybe I should be talking to somebody who can make it."

He turned back to me, his face tight. "Why are you busting my chops, Sam? I'm going to bat for you. I'm giving you a chance to get back in the game."

"And I should fall all over myself in gratitude? You want my songs but only if you get half the take. You record, you tour, you make big bucks and I get chump change."

He set his drink down and put his palms on the table, leaning in. "But it's more than you're doing now."

No argument there. I turned the empty bottle in my hands, fighting anger. "Here's the deal, Danny. I want back in the band—full member. Sunsong can pitch it as some kind of reunion in Eddie's memory. Close the circle or something; whatever. It's only one more LP. I'll supply the songs you need—my songs. Mine exclusively. And I want the same cut you get for the recording."

That was a body blow. Now it was his turn to be quiet. He looked down at the table.

"This would be a major move for me," I said. "I want to talk with my lawyer, and I want to meet with the suits."

"That will come, Sam," he said, looking me in the face again. "But I'm not going to stick out my neck then be embarrassed because you bait and switch."

"What bait and switch? I just told you the deal. What else am I going to ask for? Limo service? Free hookers for life?"

"You know there are plenty of other people who'll jump at the chance. The meter's running, Sam. Sunsong wants the LP out as soon as possible."

I set down my bottle and stood up. "Yeah, the hyenas want to eat Eddie's liver before it gets too cold."

Danny's hands clenched into fists on the table. "Do you think this is easy for me?" he said through his teeth. "My whole life's half over the edge because somebody shot Eddie and I'm left holding a big fucking bag." He caught himself and took a long breath. His hands unclenched and turned palms up in a suppliant gesture. "Look, Sam, the world might end tomorrow afternoon, but we still have to make a living in the meantime. Your melodies, my lyrics; think it over. When you're ready to talk, give me a call. Just don't wait too long." He scribbled two phone numbers on a napkin. That's my house phone and my cell. Call me."

I folded the napkin and resisted the urge to wad it up and throw it in his face. I put it in my pocket instead. What an SOB, baiting me by pulling strings to land me a prestige gig with the promise of more and then dangling a deal under my nose while I was dazzled and grateful. I imagined him telling Sunsong's execs, "I know him; let me work on him and I'll get him for us cheap and easy." I planned to stall him a few days, and if I was right, my answer wouldn't matter.

By the time I was back on my stool for the next set, Danny's table was empty.

19

I called Wendy Conn the next morning and caught her at her office. "What's up, Sam?"

"News. You should have come with me last night to the Avalanche. You could have interviewed Danny Barton."

"He was there?"

"Oh, Master of the Obvious—yeah. He made me the offer I can't refuse. Wants me to bail out his sorry ass and fill the empty slots on his CD."

"And you said?"

"I said I'd get back to him. This isn't a date for the prom. This is the rest of my life. And it cranks me that he expected me to jump for it like a trained seal."

She listened without interrupting as I recounted my conversation with Danny. "What's to think about? It's what you want isn't it?"

"It's what I wanted fifteen years ago, but suddenly being asked because that asshole is in a bind makes me feel like I just won second prize in a beauty contest."

"So take the money and run. Do your thing and retire comfortable."

"What really bothers me about it is the way Danny talked about perpetuating the Gin Sing 'brand,' like it was Drano or Listerine; just something to sell."

"Well, Sam, we all have something to sell. Sometimes we can't set the price."

"No, but we can damned sure choose who we sell it to."

She laughed. "I have to go right now, Sam. You don't need me to talk you into it or out of it. You already made up your mind. You just want to make Danny sweat for a few days before you tell him. Enjoy the moment." She hung up.

I wasn't sure what annoyed me more about the exchange, that I was so transparent to her, or as far as she was concerned that my yes or no on Danny's offer didn't matter.

A half hour later, Joe Mancini showed on my caller ID. I could all but hear him drooling over the phone. "Sam! I heard Danny Barton wants you to write for the new LP. Is that true?"

"We talked about it."

"And..."

"And what?"

"What did you say?"

"I said I'd think it over. And who told you about this anyway?"

He ignored my question. "Think it over?" Joe's voice cranked up a notch. "Sam, this is your ticket back in. It'll put you out front. You could revive your whole career."

"Indian Summer, Joe."

"What?"

"Indian Summer." I switched off the call and switched off the phone. Within an hour, he was pounding on my door. I didn't answer.

I didn't like yanking Joe around, but I knew he would force the issue, I'd have to make a decision, and I'd lose my leverage with Danny. I wanted Danny off balance. I wanted him to make a mistake, and when he did, I wanted to be ready for it.

When I turned my phone on again, I found a voice mail from Kearny in the morass of missed calls from Joe. I tried the precinct and he was out, but he called again a few minutes later.

"I got clearance to take you to Shay's place. How's tomorrow morning?"

"Suits me."

"I'll pick you up at your place at eight." He didn't ask for the address. A subtle subtext: *We know where you live.*

That afternoon I proofread and edited the Gatsby essay and that evening after a final read-through, I e-mailed it to the broker. An online payment would show up in my checking account in a day or two. Small money, but it all pays bills. Like Cotton always said, "Don't quit your day job or your night job neither."

20

Friday morning, after breakfast I shaved and showered quickly. Kearny was supposed to pick me up soon and I didn't want to keep him waiting. When I stepped out the front door of my building, he was anyway.

Kearny and another plain-clothes detective he introduced only as Lewicki drove me to Eddie's house. It was drizzling and chilly, and the Crown Vic's wipers squelched every other pass because there wasn't quite enough water on the windshield. Lewicki was short and hefty, closing on retirement, and sporting a personality like a wakened bear. His face was losing a battle with rosacea and he rubbed at his swollen nose every ten seconds or so. Everything about him suggested that retirement was just over the next hill. Lewicki was a smoker and lit up as soon as we hit the street. He flicked his ashes on the floor. I thought of Kearny and his Skoal.

"Do you guys ever use ashtrays?"

Lewicki's head turned as far as it could on his thick neck. "You see one handy?" I leaned forward and looked over the seat. There was a hole in the dashboard where the ashtray should have been. He gave a wet cough and said in a phlegm-laden voice, "Her eminence Chief Dana Whitley thinks smoking is the ninth deadly sin right after fake sick days. To 'discourage' smoking she ordered the ashtrays pulled out of all the cars. I'd use the dashboard hole, but it might catch something on fire." He added as an afterthought, "On sunny days I roll down the window."

We drove over rain-glazed streets the color of gunmetal toward Banner

Heights. Kearny and Lewicki bantered back and forth over the politics of the city budget, who was banging whom in the traffic squad, and who might win the World Series. There was no partition between the front and back seats like you'd find in a squad car, but there might as well have been for as much as I was included in the conversation. We reached Eddie's neighborhood and Kearny slowed when he turned into Albion Drive. "Okay, which one?"

I could see Kearny's eyes in the mirror and they flicked to me when he asked the question. I told him I was never in Eddie's house before, but like most good detectives, he was always throwing out a line to see if I'd slip up and bite. I didn't respond, and after a beat Lewicki said, "327, 335, there. 337."

Eddie's house was as nice as any in the upscale neighborhood, a two story brick and stone with a steep slate roof. It wasn't a mansion, but it would do. The place looked as if it may have been stylish in the early fifties, and it was well-kept like the landscaping, lots of trees and shrubs shivering in the gusting wind. I guess the continuum of star magnitude parallels that of star housing. No barbed wire, no eight-foot privacy walls, and to Kearny's irritation, no security cameras.

"Too bad there's no video," Lewicki grunted.

Kearny sighed. "That would've made it too easy."

Lewicki shook his head. "Funny, the people who don't need cameras have them all over the place. People who need them don't have any." A thought crossed my mind about causes and effects, but I held my tongue.

Kearny wheeled into the driveway, concrete, not blacktop—after all, this was Banner Heights. Macadam was probably prohibited by the Neighborhood Association. The last tatters of crime scene tape flapped and fluttered around the front door in the wind, a sad reminder of things the snooty neighbors would rather forget. We parked in front of the two-bay attached garage. I reached for the door handle to let myself out and remembered I was in a cop car. No handles in the back. Kearny popped the door and walked away, leaving me to open and close it for myself.

The wind began to blow in gusts. Lewicki, holding his tweed cap on his head with one hand, fumbled in his coat pocket for the front door key with the other. "Who ordered this friggin' weather?" The lock was stubborn and he cursed the cold rain that pelted his face. The key finally worked, and the door swung into a dark hallway.

Eddie's house wasn't opulent but way beyond what my middle-class parents would have called "comfortable." Lewicki switched on the hall chandelier and I saw a thick tongue of dark green carpet leading into the body of the place, like a model's runway. The furniture that lined the hallway was nice stuff, definitely not flea market decor.

"Studio's back here." Kearny led me past a few dim rooms and the staircase. The house had a lived-in feel; open magazines on the living room coffee table, a pair of sneakers and socks beside a fire place full of ashes; car keys and a newspaper on the hall table, frozen in the middle of life. We made a left turn through a kitchen tricked out with copper everything. Eddie had become an amateur gourmet over the years—I guess everybody needs a hobby, and one that catered to his senses seemed to suit him. Through the kitchen windows I saw a patio with a wrought iron table and chairs and a big elaborate gas grill, natural gas, not a propane tank, a grill with all the gadgets. In one corner of the patio a cedar paneled outdoor hot tub leaked wisps of steam around its cover. Eddie knew the right way to spend his money.

We left the kitchen and passed through a short hallway that had once been a cupboard into the long room behind the garage. I guessed that the room had been added to the original house by previous owners, or maybe by Eddie himself.

The studio was less dim than the rest of the house, although thick soundproofing drapes covered the windows. Overhead skylights let in the pearl grey October light, and the effect was twilight though it was ten in the morning.

By their nature, studio acoustics soak up what sound techs call "excess resonance," to eliminate even the slightest echo. Their design affects voices like an attic full of fiberglass batting. "No one's been in here since the murder," Kearny said, his voice flat. He switched on the overhead lights, long racks of fluorescents.

"Alleged murder," Lewicki jibed.

"Up yours," Kearny shot back. "Like I said, nobody's been in here since the main event, so it should be just like you saw it in the photos. Put these on so you don't leave prints." He pulled a wad of blue latex gloves from his raincoat pocket. He peeled off two and handed them to me. He offered them to Lewicki.

"Can't wear those damned things. "Got a latex allergy."

Kearny snorted. "Then keep your hands in your pockets, Lewicki. That oughta keep you entertained. And don't light up."

I started with the keyboard workstation. A full 88-key Yamaha clavinova connected to a desktop computer. "They took the laptop, why didn't they take this machine?"

Kearny frowned. "According to the tech report because it isn't wired to any Ethernet cables or phone lines, no wireless hookups, just that piano. Considering he was a musician, I guess they should've taken it too. I'll have to kick somebody's ass back at the station."

Lewicki laughed. "Yeah, nobody's perfect, including the geeks. Goddam 'de-tech-tives.'"

"We'll see if it matters." I started the computer and waited. It asked for a password, and that stalled me. "Needs a password," I said to Kearny. "I'm going to nose around and see whether Eddie left it written down anyplace." I looked in the obvious places first; the back of the tower, the underside of the workstation desk, and under the mouse pad. I imagined Eddie trying to remember it after he'd had a joint or a few hits of Jack Daniels and figured it was there someplace. I looked at the underside of the computer keyboard and all around the clavinova. No luck.

The tower had two CD drives. On some computers the drives will open if the unit's running; no login required. I wanted to check them for disks anyway, so I tried the top one. The tray slid out, but it was empty. I opened the lower one, and it was empty too, but penciled onto the tray at the back was the sequence "ZX32YW10$". The password worked, and in a minute, I was looking at the Windows desktop. "Got it."

Kearny and Lewicki stepped up and looked over my shoulder. "You got it, Dunne, but what is it?" I was "Sam" when just the two of us were talking, but "Dunne" in front of Lewicki. Did that mean I was in the club now?

Icons for a dozen or more software packages were ranked vertically on the left side of the screen: Pro Tools, Finale, Cakewalk, Q-Base, Adobe Audition, Fruit Loops, and a few others, all music programs. Thinking about the copyright forms on the desk, I pulled up Cakewalk, which printed scores, among other functions but didn't find much. Finale was next, and I found a cache of at least fifty files.

Kearny's cell phone rang and he walked away from the workstation to take the call. I waited until he was across the room to slip a thumb drive into the USB port to copy the files. I had the software at home, and I could look at them later. He spoke in a low voice to Lewicki but I could hear the words, "ballistics" and "same gun." Maybe he was talking about another case, but I doubted that. He was back looking over my shoulder in a minute.

"Anything?"

"Music files. No e-mail or downloads; nothing like that. This machine is offline, dedicated to writing and recording music. He must have kept it offline to prevent viruses or malware ruining his work."

Kearny puffed up his cheeks and blew out a long breath. "Oh well, worth a try, anyway."

For the next hour I looked at every other file I could find on the hard drive, saving the Finale files for later; nothing noteworthy. Kearny got bored watching me and started rummaging in the desk. I switched off the tower and slipped the thumb drive into my pocket. To get to the desk from the workstation, I had to step over where Eddie had fallen. The cocaine was gone, but the wood was stained a reddish brown.

I picked up the top copyright form and studied it closely. It was blank, but I was hoping it had indentations from Eddie writing on the missing third form. Columbo, call your office. No luck. My guess was he filled it in with one of the handful of felt-tipped pens that bristled out of the skull mug that grinned at me from the corner of the desk. Nothing I saw was a clue I hadn't seen before. I looked at the photo of the desktop. "Did your boys take the CD spindle?"

"Yeah. It's with the laptop, but like I told you before, they were all blanks."

The table with recording gear stood at the far end of the room behind the desk and opposite the drums and guitars. My first stop was the Rec-Tech 109. I held down the "On" button, and in a few seconds, the LCD readout glowed a muted shade of pumpkin. It said, "Insert data card." I looked at the side of the unit and saw that the gate for the card entry was closed. I slid it open; the chunky data storage card was missing.

I have to hand it to Kearny. He and Lewicki were thorough. They looked under and around every piece of furniture and equipment in the studio searching for Eddie's ring while I looked at the files and the recorder. No luck there, either.

"You know," I said, "some of those guitars are worth a couple of grand apiece. This wasn't some simple robbery."

Kearny nodded. "Yeah, that occurred to us." Irritation crept into his tone. "A common thief would have taken them and the laptop, and it doesn't look like anything was disturbed anywhere else in the house. Anything else to see here?"

"No, I guess not, but like you said, still worth a try."

As we left the studio, I looked back at the stain on the floor and thought, you won't get away, you bastard; you have my word.

On the way out we passed the living room again. "Did you check the fireplace?"

Kearny and Lewicki stopped and turned toward me in unison. Kearny gave me a three count, tilted his head back and pointing his chin at me.

They looked under and around every piece of furniture and equipment...

Then he said, with an edge in his voice. "What a novel suggestion; maybe you should be in charge, huh? Yeah, we checked the fireplace. Just simple wood and paper ashes, or maybe we should figure out whether he was burning oak or maple. That might be a clue. Whaddaya think, Lewicki?" never taking his eyes off me. He raised his eyebrows. "Any other questions?" I didn't take it personally. I was as frustrated at the dead ends as he was.

I stonewalled him; no apologies either way. In a few seconds he and Lewicki turned their backs on me dismissively and headed for the front door. That gave me the chance I needed to palm the keys from the hall table and slip them in my pocket. Eddie's house deserved a second look.

When we stepped outside, the rain ramped up and pounded hard on the roof of the car, big fat drops that were almost sleet. Lewicki carried the workstation tower half under his coat.

"When do you want me to look at the laptop?"

Kearny spoke over his shoulder as he backed the car out of the driveway. "Maybe it won't be necessary. I'll ask the techies what they think after they check out the tower. That was good how you found the password. That'll save them about three minutes."

I knew better than to push it and make Kearny suspicious. "You know me, Kearny, Mr. responsible citizen."

Lewicki snorted and flicked his ashes on the car seat. The rain poured like we should all go home and build an ark.

21

Back at my place, I shook off the rain and hung up my coat. The mail was the usual stuff. Everybody wanted money. Either they were billing me for something or trying to sell me something, or holding out their hands for donations. One envelope, bulkier than the rest, held an appeal to send money to help the children on an Indian reservation, along with a set of personalized address labels, a small notepad, and a tribal dream catcher made from sticks, yarn and feathers. My dreams were so far gone I'd never catch them, even with supernatural help. I threw the whole works in the trash.

I caught a chill out in the weather, so I changed into sweats and put on a pot of coffee. While it brewed, I foraged around the kitchen for something I could heat up for lunch. Lots of possibilities; a small Tupperware container full of Jumbalaya, half a Subway Philly cheese steak sandwich, and one lonely hot dog that probably was past the point of safety. I could make something from scratch, but I wanted to get into the Finale files.

Irritating Kearny was a calculated risk. I could have been diplomatic and said, "Did they find anything in the fireplace?" Saying, "Did you check the fireplace?" laid it on him and it got me what I wanted, his dismissal and Eddie's house key. I figured I saw everything Kearny did for the moment. There probably wasn't much on Eddie's laptop that wasn't on my thumb drive, at least nothing important. In the meantime, Kearny would leave me alone for a while. I needed the space to make a few moves of my own.

I microwaved the sub and headed for my computer.

Finale is one of the earliest computer programs to integrate MIDI technology with graphics, allowing the user to enter single notes or groups of them for audio playback as well as display on a musical staff. You could do multi-instrument tracks for recording or backup for live performance. The program could also print out anything from a single instrument line to a full orchestral score. I had used Finale since it came out in the late eighties to score and print lead sheets, a requirement for copyright, and I regularly bought the software updates.

Most of Eddie's files were named with acronyms followed by numbers, probably successive versions of a score or song. I clicked on the first one, "GBM3." The file appeared as a multi track score in scroll view, eight lines of music running from left to right off the page. I clicked on page view, and what looked like a conductor's score replaced the linear view. I skipped from page to page. GBM stood for "Gone by Monday," the tag line of the song: "I'll be there by Sunday and gone by Monday."

I switched on my desk speakers and clicked the playback control. The tune was catchy, a straight-up rocker, although the playback had the brittle, too precise feel of electronic music. No matter how sophisticated the equipment, the synthesized guitar tracks always sounded phony, but I got the feel of the song. I scrolled through the lyrics. They needed polish, but they were clever and had the necessary hook to grab the listener.

The next two files were "GBM1" and "GBM2". Next was "GBMLS", Lead Sheet. I clicked that one open, and found a standard sheet of music; melody line, chord symbols, and lyrics. The top of the page had the title "Gone By Monday" and just below that to the right, "Words and Music by Danny Barton and Eddie Shay." At the bottom of the page, a notice in both their names claimed the copyright. The copyright year was this one. This was probably one of the numbers tagged for the new CD. The next files were labeled "GBMS" for "studio" with designations for instruments; guitar, piano, percussion, bass. They were basic charts for studio musicians. Eddie was thorough. He had the whole song laid out and ready to go.

One by one, I worked through the files, reading the scores, listening to the playback. Some of them I ran from the earliest version through the latest, fascinated with the way Eddie's ideas evolved. Most of Danny's lyrics were boilerplate. Eddie's artistry made them dance. For a moment I thought maybe I should sell my soul and take Danny's offer. This music would sell, and probably sell big, the publicity from Eddie's murder aside. My songs on the same CD could sell right along with them.

I shook off the idea and for the next two hours I plowed on until I reached a pair of files named "YNM" and" YNMLS", the only two with that acronym. They were dated September 13th and 28th, respectively. I clicked up the later one and a lead sheet showed on the screen. YNM stood for "You and Me." The songwriter tag and copyright notices were in Eddie's name only. I clicked the playback control and heard a familiar melody. I had to remind myself to breathe. I scrolled through the lyrics, and in just the right place with just the right notes were the words, "You and me." You and Me: Carry On.

I took a long, slow breath and said in a low voice. "Got you, you sonofabitch."

If Danny Barton didn't pull the trigger on Eddie and Lottie, he aimed the shooter. Time to talk to the bad boys. I needed Wendy's eyes and her intuition. I also needed to see how she'd work a scene she didn't control. I got her on her cell. "Busy tonight?"

"Nothing I can't postpone. What's up?"

"Field trip. Ever go in the East End?"

"Only when somebody's murdered. What's there?"

"Bendik's."

"I've driven past it—at high speed."

"Come over to my place around nine. We'll take my car; it's less likely to be stolen."

"Nine," she said. There was a pause and she added, "Anything for a story. Should I wear my Kevlar socks?"

As I snapped my phone shut, I decided that Wendy Conn was maybe the bravest woman I ever met, or the craziest. Either way, she'd do.

It was time to tell her what I knew and what I suspected about Danny. I'd reached the point that I had to trust somebody, and between her and Kearny, she won. If things blew up and something happened to me, she could print a story that would point the cops at him. I chose her because Kearny followed a set of rules that were less pragmatic. Also, I couldn't count on Kearny's enthusiasm to run with what I had, all circumstantial. I needed hard proof, and if Kearny went after Danny now, he'd lawyer up and maybe get away.

I didn't doubt that I could kill Danny myself, and it might even be worth it, but I'd end up in a cell for the rest of my days. If I could put him there instead, that might be the best outcome. To do that, I needed solid evidence; to find that evidence, I had to step into the shade.

22

Wendy showed up a few minutes early. She was wearing a pair of tight black jeans tucked into knee high boots and a light leather jacket over a loose denim shirt. I was still in my bare feet. "Huckleberry Finn?" she quipped.

"Yeah. I'll be right with you as soon as I find my straw hat. Have a seat." While I laced my Doc Martens, I told her about the copyright forms, but instead of annoyance, she showed something bordering on admiration.

"Well played, Sam, but you don't know what Eddie might have done with the form. What if he mailed it between the time the picture was taken and the time he was killed? How could you find out?"

"It takes weeks for the Copyright Office to process electronic forms, let alone hard copy stuff. It's public information once it's registered, but in the meantime…" I shrugged.

"Besides, the form doesn't prove much, does it?"

"It might. There's something else." I walked over to the desk and clicked my computer's mouse. The desktop woke up and I opened Finale. "Listen to this song." I clicked Play and a simple piano line flowed out of the speakers.

In a few seconds Wendy recognized the melody. "That's 'Carry On,' right?"

"That's a song called 'You and Me'; it's Eddie's song. Come look at the screen."

She leaned toward the monitor, her face blue from its glow. "It's all in his name. No mention of Danny Barton."

"Right. Read the lyrics; they're different. And when you click on the file properties," which I did. "Look at the date."

She let out a breath she'd been holding. "Holy shit."

"My thoughts exactly. I'd call that a motive. Lottie mentioned a breakout song that Eddie played for her. I'm betting this is it."

"But you said he can't read music. Wouldn't this be worthless to him?"

"A lead sheet would but not a demo. Lottie said he played a demo for her; that means he had it recorded and Danny could have picked the song up by ear if he had a copy. I didn't find "You and Me" on the computer tower in any other format. Kearny's boys found a stack of empty CDs, so maybe Danny grabbed any that were marked. That leaves the digital recorder, where he might have done a multi-track demo. The recording could still be on the missing data card. That would explain why Danny was after the same model recorder, to play the song from the data card."

"And if Lottie heard Danny play 'Carry On' on *Jumpstart* and recognized it, she'd know Danny stole the song . . ."

"Motive."

She nodded slowly, turning to look me in the face. "You may be right, but how could we prove it?"

I smiled at her use of "we." As of that moment, she was on my team, not Kearny's. "We do a little field work. Ready to step into the grey zone?"

She was quiet for a minute, staring at nothing, lips clamped and eyes to the side, weighing the options. "I have to ask; do you suppose you think Danny's guilty because you want him to be?"

I slipped a hand in my pocket. "If you listen close, you'll hear the click of rosary beads, and I'm not a Catholic. Even if I'm wrong about the murders, I'm right about the song. We'll get him either way. Are you in?"

She looked me in the face and instead of that wicked grin of hers; I got a look of determination. "Let's do it."

• • •

I have a soft spot in my heart for Bendik's, even though it's one of the roughest bars where I've ever played a guitar. Every town has one place where the misfits, outlaws and people on the fringe gather and operate under their own twisted code. In Hanniston, Bendik's was it. I had worked there with different bands over the years, and while the rest of the world evolved, Bendik's never changed. When I walk in there, I flash on the bar scene from *Star Wars.* You think by the time you're legal age you've seen every kind of weirdo, degenerate and bad actor breathing, but every time you walk into Bendik's you find something new.

The bar is in the East End, the neighborhood itself a poster child for urban blight; streets of chain link fences and boarded facades. The one-story building is the old Bendik garment factory that made military uniforms in World War II then segued to industrial clothes with company logos in the fifties and sixties before the company went tits up. The building stood idle for a few years, then somebody decided the neighborhood needed one more bar. Mac Jacobs, the new owner, started with just the front half of the building, then expanded to the back half as Hanniston's misfits found a new home and dropped anchor. Mac kept the old Bendik name and never bothered to change the sign.

The windows facing the street were glass block, primarily to minimize replacement. Harsh flood lights shone from above, not on the sign but on the sidewalk where two big bikers guarded the door. There was no need to light the sign. People who would go to Bendik's found it almost by instinct. The cops had an unofficial treaty with Mac; they never came in unless somebody died. His bouncers pretty much settled issues without outside help. The payback: Bendik's kept a lot of baddies off the streets at night.

I parked the van in the gravel lot. "Shove your purse under the seat. You won't need it."

Wendy nodded.

"And when we go in, don't talk to anybody and avoid eye contact."

"I know the drill. I've been in bad places before."

"Not like this one." I took the bills out of my wallet and locked the wallet in the console. I divided the cash into four parts and put them in different pockets.

Wendy eyed me. "What's that all about?"

"Somebody picks your pocket or knocks you on the head, they don't get it all."

We crossed the street and stepped through an uncountable rank of Harleys propped at the curb. The doormen eyed us up and down. The one on the left had severe acne and wore a Confederate Flag bandanna; the one on the right was bare headed, his black hair slicked back into a short ponytail that looked like he groomed it with motor oil. Aviator shades perched on his nose.

Pony tail nodded to the urban rebel, who opened the blank steel door to let us inside. The blast of heat, music and smoke was enough to knock you over. I stepped over the threshold and into what looked like Dante's Inferno. The brightest lights in the room were the red bar neons, which made the joint look like a foundry pit.

Inside the door, Frankie sat behind his table collecting the five-dollar cover charge. Frankie—I've never heard his real name if he has one—is short for his nickname, which I'm sure you can guess. When he stands up, the rest of us feel like midgets. His face has a dozen scars, the worst a thick white seam from the side of his nose all the way to his chin, giving him a look like a double hare-lip. His forearms, as thick as four-by-fours and crawling with jailhouse tatts, rested on either side of a pile of bills like a small haystack, daring anybody to grab for it. He looked at me for a second and said, "Dunne."

I nodded and returned the greeting. "Frankie." I handed him a ten and he dropped it on the pile and raised his chin in acknowledgement. He nodded and smiled at Wendy, the way a grizzly bear smiles at a fawn.

We shouldered through the standing crowd to the bar. Jill the barmaid came over, smiling. Her face was glossy with sweat in the bar lights. "Hey, Sam, long time gone," she shouted over the noise.

"Hi, Jill. Two longnecks. Leave 'em capped."

Her smile evaporated. She hesitated for a second then nodded. "Four bucks." She turned to get the beers and I pulled a five out of my shirt pocket. Jill came back with the beers. "Keep the change, hon."

I handed Wendy one of the bottles and she leaned up and shouted in my ear, "Why are the caps on?"

It annoys me when I'm at a concert or a club and people yell in my ear to be heard over the music. Besides that, it's painful. I leaned down and said in a normal voice, "If you get right up on my ear and talk normally, I can hear you fine. You don't have to shout."

She nodded.

I leaned in again. "The bottles aren't to drink; they're to swing if we have a problem. Jill won't do that for most people, but they know me in here. Stick close." We wormed our way through the crowd, hard-eyed men and harder-eyed women in denim and leather. Bendik's was a kind of resort for vacationing Carnies and ex cons.

In certain places, you learn a way of looking around people, not at them, if you want to avoid trouble. You register their presence, take their measure, and assess their threat in a glance, but your eyes pass over them like quicksilver, never lingering long enough to make them self-conscious. The wisdom of Brian Setzer: "Look at me once, look at me twice, look at me again there's gonna be a fight." People in Bendik's never got past their second look.

Wendy wore an impassive face, looking almost bored as we moved through the tables. She handled it well. Past the front bar and table area, Bendik's opened into a huge dance floor with a six-foot-high platform at the far end and a second bar to the right. Tables ringed the floor, and tonight it was packed. Blood Lightning was playing.

The stage was flanked by scaffolds with arena-sized speakers and colored spots. A cloud of smoke floated between the heads of the crowd and the high ceiling, part tobacco, part reefer, and probably a little crack, changing colors with the flashing lights. On the stage, Blood Lightning was tearing through a cover of AC/DC's "Dirty Deeds Done Dirt Cheap," and the room pulsed with the music like some primordial heartbeat. The bass punched you in the chest. The drummer played with a pair of sticks in each hand, and his rim shots ricocheted off the inside of your skull.

In the center of the stage, the lead guitarist launched into an extended solo, fingers flying up and down the neck and ripping through the room like a blade. "That's the man we're here to see," I told Wendy. "That's Razor."

Tall, lean, rawboned and wiry in jeans and a dark sleeveless T-shirt, Razor strutted back and forth across the stage like a barnyard rooster while he cranked out riff after riff. He sneered through two days' worth of stubble and his lank blonde hair whipped around his face as he jerked his head from one side to the other. The crowd on the dance floor surged like waves in a hurricane.

I stole a glance at Wendy. In spite of herself she was caught up in the uninhibited spectacle. This was a long way from a Jackson Browne concert. The song ended to cheers from the crowd. "And now," Razor snarled in to the mic, "Let's hear it for her majesty, the Duchess!"

From the back of the stage, a tall, big-boned woman in leather pants and bustier strode onto the stage to more cheers. Her black hair cascaded almost to her waist, and her sensuous lips were painted that shade of fresh blood you find in your First Grade Crayola box.

"Who's she?"

"One of the most amazing people you'll ever see."

Duchess grabbed the stand and didn't bother taking the mic out of the collar. She looked out into the crowd and shouted, "How you all doin' out there tonight?" Whoops, whistles and hand clapping answered her. "All right! Let's tear this mother down!" She clapped her hands over her head and the crowd picked it up. In a minute she gave her hair a toss signaling the drummer, who rolled into Etta James' "Tell Mama."

While the band ran the song's signature intro, Duchess opened those red lips wide enough to swallow the mic and belted out a raw vibrato scream that lasted five measures and gave me chills. The crowd cheered louder.

Duchess ripped through the song as a wild-eyed mob jammed the front of the stage, reaching for her. Razor hunched over his guitar as he played his solo, and she arched her back over him, mouth open with pure lust.

Wendy nudged me. "That's the closest thing I've ever seen to sex with clothes on."

"It gets better."

The song ended with a long shrieking chord and pounding drum rolls. Duchess held the mic stand with two hands over her head like a barbell. Before the cheers died down, Razor cranked out another opening riff and the crowd exploded again when it recognized Bonnie Raitt's "Love Me Like A Man." Duchess strutted across the stage like a panther in heat to grab the mic, and when the band got quiet, so did the crowd in rapt attention. Her voice dripped honey laced with smoke and bourbon; every man in the room was sweating, and their women understood because they were sweating too.

After two verses, she reached into her bustier and pulled out a blues harp. The crowd went crazy as she and Razor faced off. She'd blow a sinuous riff on the harmonica, and Razor would answer with a fluid cascade of notes. At the peak of the song when the band stops and she sings the tag line, she got as far as "Love me like…" and just stopped. Nobody breathed. Duchess looked at the floor, looked at Razor, looked at the floor again and said, "Oh, fuck it."

She turned away from the mic and crossed the stage to Razor, grabbed a handful of his hair and gave him a kiss so full of passion and violence that it about tore his lips off. The drummer gave three flams and the band kicked back in, finishing the song while Duchess ground her pelvis into Razor's thigh. Applause thundered.

Wendy elbowed me. "She one of your old flames?"

I smiled at the memory. "For a day and a half. She chews up men like candy, but I think she met her match with Razor."

We moved closer to the stage as the crowd allowed, and half way through the band's version of "Combination of the Two" Razor spotted me. I put the tip of my index finger at the corner of my eye. He read the signal and gave an almost imperceptible nod.

Four songs later, the band took a break. As he walked off, Razor glanced at me and flicked his head to the left side of the stage.

I tugged at Wendy's jacket and led her off the dance floor toward the backstage entrance. "Now what?"

"We wait." We stood at a curtained doorway in a partition between the edge of the stage and the wall. Behind the curtain the old factory offices had been converted to dressing and party rooms for the bands. A guy the size of a refrigerator with a beard like a paintbrush stood guard. He didn't speak and neither did we. A chainsaw concerto of heavy metal blasted through the sound system; Muzak for the psychotic.

In a minute, Razor came through the portal wiping his face with a towel and tossed it through the curtains. He paused to light a cigarette and strode up to us with the same reptilian grace he plied onstage. "Sam Dunne."

"Still smokin' unfiltered Luckies?"

"I can only find 'em in Kentucky these days. Heard they make 'em in Switzerland now."

"Razor, meet Wendy. Wendy, meet Razor." He nodded toward her and his eyelids lowered. If she felt undressed, the effect was intentional.

He gestured to the bar and said, "Let's get a beer." His eyes flicked to the bottles we were holding. "One you can drink." He led us through a crowd that parted like the Red Sea. Two guys stepped in Razor's path. The bigger one was stocky, dressed in outdated grunge garb; flannel shirt, Doc Marten boots and a White Freightliner ball cap. I couldn't hear what he was saying, but judging by his face, it wasn't friendly. I moved between them and Wendy, but she edged around me anyway, the reporter in her wanting to see it all.

Razor said something back to the grunger, who took a swing. Razor's cigarette exploded into a shower of orange sparks, and the fight was on. Razor gave him a couple of hard body shots and grabbed him by the throat with his left hand and the crotch with his right. He twisted his hands and the grunger would have screamed if he could have gotten any air out of his mouth. Big as the guy was, Razor lifted him and body slammed him onto a table, scattering bottles and people. I saw the grunger's buddy edge behind Razor and I stepped in his direction. He caught me watching him, not the fight and changed his mind.

In a few seconds, five bouncers with ball bats bulldozed through the crowd. Razor let go of the grunger and jumped back, hands in the air and open. Back on his feet, the grunger rushed Razor, swinging his fists and shouting. One of the bouncers swung his bat like a golf club and swept the guy's feet from under him. He crashed to the floor and two of the others dragged him away by his ankles. His friend was smart enough not to protest or follow. He disappeared into the sea of people. I turned back to

Wendy. She was holding her bottle by the neck, eyes sweeping the crowd. I was right. She had some spine. She'd do.

Razor peeled a hundred dollar bill off a roll from his pocket and threw it on the table he'd trashed. "Drink up. Sorry for the upset." Wendy stared incredulously as people applauded.

"What was that all about?" I said to Razor as we sidled up to the bar.

"Better you don't know." Razor answered. "So what's up?"

"Job."

He stared into the mirror behind the bar. We all got drafts and I leaned in so he could hear me but no one else could. Though he never looked at me, even in the mirror, he paid close attention to every word I said. At the same time he was aware of every person and everything around him. I sketched out my case on Danny and my plan to deal with it. He listened, his expression never changing. Finally he nodded.

I pulled a wad of bills from my waistband and set it on the bar, covering it with my hand. "Expenses."

He shook his head. "Hang onto it. If you're wrong, we'll settle up after. If you're right, this one's on me. Lottie was a friend to all of us." He looked past me to Wendy, who was leaning back against the bar and watching our backs. "And the babe?"

"She's the shiner." Wendy's eyes flicked to me but she didn't speak.

He nodded, and turned back to the mirror. I handed him a business card with my phone number. He looked at it and handed it back. "Got it. I'd give you mine, but it changes from day to day." He laughed. "Back to work, Sam. I'll be in touch." He turned to Wendy. "Glad you came." He gave her a predatory smile. "I'm sure I'll see you again sometime." Razor stepped away from the bar and headed for the stage.

I finished my beer and said, "Let's go before one of these animals decides he doesn't like my looks or likes yours."

Wendy didn't say a word until we got to the parking lot. I thumbed the lock button on my key fob and we climbed into the van. She pulled a hank of her hair around to her nose and sniffed it. "Ugh. You stand in there three nights in a row and you'll end up in a cancer ward. No cigarette required."

"Occupational hazard of walking on the wild side. So, how did you like Bendik's?"

"Scared me shitless, and I'm not ashamed to admit it."

I started the van and backed out of my space. "No shame in being smart. You handled yourself well, by the way."

"Thanks. I've had a little practice."

"But there are worse places. It's all in knowing how to behave. Even Hell has rules."

"Why did Razor step back with his hands up? I thought somebody pulled a gun on him."

"Protocol. In Bendik's the bouncers take out anybody who's swinging to stop trouble fast before it spreads. They don't discriminate. Razor held his hands up and open; no fists, no weapons. No resistance."

"And the other guy?"

"Maybe he didn't know the rules, or he was too hot to pound Razor to think about it. I'd guess his friend will take him to the emergency room after the bouncers use him for batting practice.

"Jesus."

"Jesus has nothing to do with it. It's all about action and consequences."

We drove through late night streets that were eerily empty and quiet after the noise and crush of the bar. But on the other side of the windshield, between the street lights, everything bad on the planet was waiting, ready to pounce. Wendy was quiet for a minute then said, "I think I know, but I'll ask anyway. What's a shiner?" Her hearing was better than I thought.

"Face man talk for a lure, a distraction to keep the mark busy while the plot hatches."

She nodded. "And who am I going to distract, as if I didn't know?"

"Who else? Danny boy."

"And what exactly is Razor? Some kind of hit man?"

"Nope, he's a burglar."

Her mouth formed a silent Oh.

"You interview Danny; maybe over dinner to stretch it."

"And while I'm 'shining' Danny..."

"Razor and I go fishing."

"But Danny won't take my calls. How do I set up an interview?"

"You didn't call the right number. Call Sunsong's publicity people. They'll welcome the ink. They want to ride the dead Eddie horse for all it's worth. Danny's running scared with them because his contract's up and a lot depends on this last LP. They clap, he'll jump."

"You've really thought this through, haven't you?"

"The Devil is in the details."

"You missed your calling, Sam. You shouldn't be writing songs, you should be writing murder mysteries."

I snorted. "Don't be ridiculous."

23

When we got close to my apartment, Wendy leaned forward and pulled her purse from its hiding place. She started rummaging through it. "I haven't checked my messages for a couple of hours." She buttoned on her cell phone and the screen bathed her face in a ghostly blue light.

From the corner of my eye I watched her punch buttons with her thumbs faster than I could type on a full-sized keyboard with all my fingers. She held the phone to her ear and listened, punched a few more buttons and listened some more. "Kearny left a message. I have to call him right now. Don't talk or even cough." She looked at me to make sure I understood.

"Got it." She was keeping Kearny and me in separate compartments, but that was okay with me. I wanted us in separate compartments too.

She entered a number and held the phone to her ear. In a few seconds, she said, "Mike? Wendy. You called?"

There was a pause and I saw her face change, become more focused. "When was this?" Another pause. "I'm in the car right now. Let me call you back in a few minutes when I can write it all down. Okay? That's great news, Mike. And thanks." She clicked off the call. "You won't believe this, Sam. Kearny's got a murder suspect in a holding cell right now, and it's not Danny Barton, it's some guy named Grooms."

• • •

Lavalle "Blue Smoke" Grooms was a rolling dealer, a small fish imported from Chicago by an uncle higher up the food chain. He wore six button suits and a white fedora, and he dealt out of his car, a midnight blue Escalade. Grooms sold to a limited clientele of affluent and connected people. He was too flamboyant to ignore but too small for the immediate attention of the narcotics team, and in one way he performed a public service; he delivered to a lot of upscale clients on their home turf and kept them from being mugged, murdered, or carjacked buying their coke in the East End.

Tonight, Blue Smoke's number was up. A tail light burned out in the Escalade. A patrol car on routine rounds spotted it and put on the flashers. If Lavalle had kept his cool, he might have finessed the cops and gotten away clean, but earlier in the evening he broke the dealer's number one rule: don't sample your product on the job. Whether he acted from panic or coke-fueled bravado doesn't matter. He bolted.

The dashboard cam footage from the cop cruiser was all over the TV news and the internet the next day. Peckinpah couldn't have directed a better action sequence. Seventy miles an hour doesn't seem like much tooling down the Turnpike, but on city streets with cross traffic, garbage trucks and pedestrian islands, it's a tricky proposition. Blue Smoke missed his calling; he should have driven for NASCAR, or maybe Joie Chitwood. What resulted was a wild demolition derby as he sideswiped four or five cars, took out a mailbox and a hydrant, and barely missed T-boning a pickup truck at an intersection. He tried for the interstate but his luck ran out on the ramp when he slipped between a tractor trailer hauling a Cat D-9 and the Jersey barrier.

The trucker, a redneck from Kentucky named Joe Shackleton, saw the headlights coming fast in his mirrors with the flashers close behind and squeezed left. Blue Smoke was going too fast to avoid the crunch and ended up wedged between the semi and the concrete. His doors were all blocked, and he was making an exit through the sunroof when Shackleton climbed over the Caddy's hood and whacked him on the head with a lug wrench. Pure Hollywood.

The cops found an unregistered pistol stashed under the driver's seat. Strike one. A storage compartment under the back seat of Blue Smoke's car turned up a respectable inventory of recreational drugs and another handgun. Strike two. When the officers kicked back the passenger seat, something shiny gleamed in the carpet. It was a silver ring in the shape of a rattlesnake's head. Strike three.

Because the chase footage went viral on the internet, Fox, CNN and MSNBC ran with the story. In Harrigan's, in Starbucks, and anywhere else there was a TV set, I saw Kearny standing behind Dana Whitley, the Chief of Police. The same clip from the steps of the Precinct building ran every half hour. It was windy, blowing Whitley's usually perfect blonde coif askew and flapping Kearny's necktie like a pennant. She read from a prepared statement that she could probably have memorized in the fifteen seconds it took to deliver it. "We now have a suspect in custody for the murder of Edmund Shay. Because the investigation is ongoing, I can make no further comment at this time." No mention of Lottie. The clip was bracketed by scenes from the chase and followed by Lavalle's perp walk. That and meaningless speculation in the studio, laced with background on Eddie's murder that didn't seem worth running when it happened. If everybody else is talking about it, let's talk about it too.

Channel Three hung the nickname "the Diamond Dealer" on Grooms,

whacked him on the head with a lug wrench

alluding to his ritzy clientele, and you could hear toilets flush all over Bell Heights. The media and the cops would try to hang Eddie's murder on Grooms, no doubt in my mind. Razor couldn't call me soon enough. The meter was running, and I had to get my plans moving before the cops said, "Amen" and Danny walked.

24

I dodged Joe Mancini's calls for two days because I wanted to keep Danny dangling just a little bit longer, but I realized it was probably a bad idea. I hadn't been thinking clearly. Working with Danny would put me closer to him, and though the idea made my skin crawl, I realized that it might give me a better shot at bringing him down. Just like Lavalle Grooms' arrest, my taking his offer might lull him into a false sense of security. Let him think the stars were aligned. I called Joe.

"Sam! Jesus Christ! I've been trying to reach you for days. Where the hell have you been?"

"And hello to you too, Joe. I've been busy thinking things over."

"Please tell me you told Danny yes."

"No, I didn't." There was a long silence at the other end of the line. I imagined Joe checking to see that his gun was loaded and putting the muzzle in his mouth. "You're my agent. That's your job. You tell him yes."

I heard him let out a long breath. "Don't do things like that to me, Sam. I swear my heart stopped."

"You make the calls. Sunsong's on a tight schedule and they not only need me, they want me. Otherwise Danny wouldn't have come slithering around."

"You're right, Sam. Jack Paine from Sunsong's been calling me three times a day. They want the LP done and out before people forget about Eddie's murder. God those guys are cold."

"All the more reason to work them over. I told Danny what I wanted; a full share of the royalties, to play on the recording, exclusive credit for any of my songs on the LP, and my membership in Gin Sing restored."

"The only point Sunsong can't decide is putting you back in the band. That's up to Danny and the lawyers to sort out, but if I push it hard to Paine, he'll lean on Danny. I'll see what I can do." Like most people who make a living brokering others, he made more when I made more. "I'll see what I can do" meant he was going for Sunsong's nuts.

"You handle it, Joe. I know you'll get the best deal for all of us."

"Not all of us, Sam, both of us. Do you need anything for this weekend?"

"Yeah. I want to bring Wendy Conn with me. She's covering Eddie's murder for the *Sentinel* and it got her interested in Gin Sing as background for a feature piece. See if the hostess objects."

"Are you kidding? Lois and Don'll eat it up."

"And while I'm thinking about it, mention to Sunsong's P.R. crew that she's tried to contact Danny for the same story and he's brushed her off. See if they'll nudge him a little."

"Anything else you want, like the sun, moon, and stars?"

"Only if they're tax free."

I thumbed off my phone while Joe was still laughing and stared at the wall. Let them all think I was selling out. I hated the idea, but if it helped nail Danny, I was willing to swallow my pride in the short run. In the end, everybody would know why I gave in. In the meantime, I just had to hold my nose and play it right.

25

Razor's call came around 4:30. "Check your mail."

I rode the elevator to the lobby and unlocked my mailbox. In it was an envelope. In it was a ticket for the Wildcats, the local minor league baseball team. In three hours I'd be in the upper deck of Carson Stadium but I wouldn't be watching the game.

Wendy called while I was in the shower and left a voice mail. "Call me," was all she said. When I did, she answered on the second ring. I could hear keyboards clacking and voices. She was in the newsroom.

"Sam, we need to talk. I have some things to tell you."

"When and where?"

"I can be at your place around five-thirty. Will that do?"

"Yeah. Come on over. I have some things to tell you too."

I got dressed and decided not to make dinner. Nothing tastes quite like a ballpark hot dog.

• • •

Wendy showed up on time, looking strung out. She'd switched the black jeans and boots for her regular jeans and running shoes but kept the denim shirt, as if she'd changed in a hurry. Her eyes were red-rimmed from contact lenses in too long. She walked past me and flopped on the sofa.

"Did you sleep at all last night?"

"Not a minute." She tilted her head back and shut her eyes. "I've been running back and forth between the paper and the precinct since I left you. I can't believe the cable networks are on this."

"And it's all bullshit."

"Maybe, and maybe not. The ring, the coke, it adds up in its own way."

"What about Grooms?"

"They're sweating him. He says he never saw the ring before and he never knew Eddie. By the way, Kearny hasn't slept either."

"Lot of that goin' around. Any connection between Grooms and Eddie?"

"Nothing solid yet, but Kearny thinks it's just a matter of time 'til they find one. After all, Grooms was the delivery boy for plenty of high-end people. They're going through his cell phone backlog. He erased everything before eight o'clock last night."

"If he dumps his calls regularly, he won't have any from the night of the murder."

"They can subpoena his cell phone records, but that'll take a day or two. And I'm guessing most people who called him wouldn't use traceable phones anyway. I sneaked a look at the call list while Kearny wasn't looking; but no names yet, just numbers. Maybe we'll find out Eddie was doing coke and bought from him."

I thought about that for a minute. Sometimes people drift across boundaries, even for the shortest time and fall down a well they can't escape. "Maybe, but with no prints or a solid link between the two, Kearny's evidence is as circumstantial as ours."

"Except for the ring."

"And it's Eddie's ring for sure?"

She nodded. "Looks like it." She squeezed the muscles at the base of her skull. "Even if Grooms' customers would testify where he was on the third, and that's not likely, there's still the time factor. Between seven and midnight, he would have been all over town. He could have killed Eddie as a stop along the way. By the way, both the guns in the car were nine millimeter. No .38; no murder weapon, at least in this case."

"So, Grooms is running neck-and-neck with Danny."

"But Kearny doesn't know that. Maybe it's time to tell him."

"Maybe not. If Danny thinks he's home free, he'll let his guard down."

She massaged her eyes with the heels of her hands. "You're right. And even if he's innocent, Grooms will get five to ten for the drugs and another two or three for the rodeo last night. They aren't letting him out any time soon. He's lawyered up and clammed up; so far, no bail."

"So even if we did put Kearny onto Danny, it won't change Grooms's scenery much in the short run. And that still leaves Lottie as a loose end."

Then she surprised me with a side of her I hadn't seen. Maybe she was just cranky from fatigue. "Grooms is a freakin' cockroach anyway. Let him sit." She opened her eyes wide, blinked a few times, shook her head like a dog shaking off rain, and without looking at me said, "Got any ice cubes?"

26

Carson Stadium is a small baseball park built in the sixties when baseball was a bigger deal than it is today, pushed aside by the NFL, the NBA, and MMA. The home team, the Wildcats, was a farm team for the Indians and enjoyed an enthusiastic fan base when they were winning, but not this year. It was the tail end of a slow season. The parking lot was half empty when I got out of the van although the game was already going.

I bought a hot dog, nachos and a beer at a concession stand and headed for my seat. My ticket planted me in an upper tier section with a sparse crowd. I found my seat, watched the game, and enjoyed my junk food. Two innings later, Razor sat down beside me. He was wearing khaki slacks and a golf shirt under a windbreaker. He was clean shaven and his hair was tucked under a Wildcats ball cap; he looked like just another fan.

The stadium was an ideal place for a meet. Even if somebody sat close by, he couldn't hear us over the noise from game. Razor watched the play for a while and finally said, "You didn't tell me your shiner's a reporter." He stared straight ahead and so did I. There was no anger in his voice; a simple statement of fact.

"Didn't seem relevant."

"Everything is relevant."

"What's to report? That she's acting as an accomplice to a break-in?" One of the home boys got a base hit and the crowd cheered.

"That's this week. How about next month on a slow news day? I can see the headlines now: 'Heavy Metal Rocker – Master Criminal'. How much does she know?"

"No details. I see your point, but it was either trust her or trust the cops. I needed somebody who could shine Danny."

A bad call from the home plate umpire brought boos and jeers from the crowd.

He took a pull from his beer. "You'll understand if I don't come along for the ride."

Razor made sense; he always did. "Got it." I started to get up and he caught my sleeve.

"Stay put. Give me your phone." I did, and he flipped it open. I watched as his thumbs flew over the buttons. He opened the memo function and punched in a set of numbers from memory. He closed the phone, wiped it on his shirt and handed it back. "I called in a favor. Unless Danny changes his alarm codes in the meantime, punch those numbers in the pad by the door and you're in free. You have one minute before the alarms go off."

I nodded. Razor went on. "Danny's back door has an older Kwik Set deadbolt about the same as your apartment's lock. You can't open that one with a credit card." He handed me a small snap button case a little bigger than a wallet. "Practice, practice, practice."

I slipped the case into my pocket without looking at it. "Thanks, man."

He turned to me. "We all do what we can. Get him, Sam."

"Bet on it. You first or me?"

He jerked his head to the side. "Go ahead. I'll stick around a while." I stood up to leave, and he picked up the box with what was left of my nachos and leaned back in his seat. "I love these guys."

I waited until I got back to the van to open the case Razor gave me. It held a set of lock picks.

27

I didn't want to risk my neighbors walking off the elevator and catching me picking my own lock, so I decided to wait until they left for work to start training. I was pretty good with car locks when I was younger. I worked summers through college as a maintenance man at one of the state parks, and at least twice a week I earned a tip when some tourist locked his keys in the trunk. I knew the right people and I probably could have graduated to car thief with a little mentoring, but I decided that path was too risky in the long run. No matter how careful you are, when you misbehave long enough or often enough, chance catches up with you and you get nailed. But it was great theater the morning after a romantic evening for my girlfriend to find a rose on the front seat of her locked car.

The set of lock picks Razor gave me was a basic one, six of the most common picks and a tension wrench, not exactly pro tools, but as he said, the Lock on Danny's front door was nothing complex. I've opened doorknob locks with either a bobby pin or a paperclip in the past. Dead bolts are a little bit tougher. I opened my door and checked the corridor. No people, no sound. The door opened inward, so I swung it in at ninety degrees to the hallway. I pulled my desk chair over and then changed my mind. I knelt down instead. I wouldn't have a chair on Danny's porch. I watched some You Tube videos the night before to refresh my memory as to technique, and I felt ready to try it.

Key locks are simple mechanisms complicated by multiplication. A set of pins project downward and prevent the lock cylinder from rotating and retracting the deadbolt. The more pins, the more complex the lock. The teeth of your key push a set of pins into alignment at what locksmiths call the "shear" point, allowing the plug to rotate. Line up the pins and open the lock.

I pushed the tension wrench as far as it would go into the bottom of the keyhole opposite the pins and used a C-rake to work the pins. Then I used a short hook to nudge them into place. A good sense of touch is vital to picking a lock. Keeping a little bit of tension on the wrench, I could feel each pin as it slipped into line. Once I had the pins in place, I twisted the tension wrench clockwise, and the deadbolt retracted.

Unlocking was half the job. If Danny's house had a spring lock knob on any exterior door I could reset the deadbolt with the inside twist key and go out locking the other door behind me. If it didn't, or the lock I opened was keyed from both sides, I'd have to use the pick set to relock the door so he didn't come home and find it open. I worked the pins again and twisted the wrench the other way. The deadbolt slid out of its recess.

I took off my watch and set it on the floor beside me, waiting for the second hand to hit twelve. I worked the lock in a little under three minutes; too much time. I'd be visible from the alley that ran behind the houses if a car went by, and maybe some neighbor taking out his trash would spot me from his backyard. Razor could open a lock with his tools as fast as most people would with a key. Like he said, practice, practice, practice, and that's what I did for a good chunk of the morning.

I was missing pieces of the puzzle. Tossing Danny's house might shake loose one or two, but I figured Lavalle Grooms must be sitting on one of them. I don't move in his circles financially or otherwise, and though the black community sees me as "ofay but okay," the wagons were circled around Blue Smoke, and I wasn't about to get an audience on my own recognizance. It was time to talk to Cotton.

28

The Regent Hotel is a fixture in Hanniston, an old style establishment from an age when each hotel had a distinct personality, unlike today's cookie cutter high rises, like the Holiday Inns and Sheratons. The Regent takes up most of a city block with its Sullivan architecture, and though it is now dwarfed by its newer neighbors, corporate towers of glass and steel, the Regent maintains a stately presence that newer buildings will never capture. The vintage marble, wood, and brass inside smell of old money and big money, and stepping into its lobby is like stepping into a 40s movie. You almost expect to see Spencer Tracy and Katharine Hepburn step off the elevator or Humphrey Bogart walk out of the bar.

I didn't see Bogart in the bar, but I did find Cotton. The Cotton Breakiron Trio was nestled in an alcove at the far end of the room: Cotton on tenor, Bobby Briton on piano, and Jack Stubbs on the upright bass. They were dressed in suits and playing "Blue Bossa" when I came in, Cotton blowing a sweet, soulful tone that makes any song his property in the here and now. His shaved head shone in the lights as bright as the brass of his sax.

I ordered a Heineken and told the bartender, a cute little blonde, to run me a tab. She brought my beer, and I ignored the glass she brought with it. I turned on the stool and leaned, back to the bar so that I could see the stage while I drank from the bottle. "Blue Bossa" ended to light applause and someone from one of the front tables said something I couldn't hear. Cotton smiled about a foot wide and nodded at the request. Stubbs kicked off a syncopated bass line that I knew. The trio launched into "Green Dolphin Street," and many in the crowd clapped in recognition. They played the song end to end then started trading solos. Where Cotton and Stubbs were animated, Britton barely moved anything but his hands up and down the baby grand sounding as if he had a finger for every key on the piano. His head moved just a little from side to side marking his rhythm, his shock of white hair glowing in the colored spots.

Cotton jumped back in for a minute, and then it was Stubbs's turn. I've always thought that most bass players wrestle with the instrument more than they collaborate with it, but not Stubbs. The bass responded to his huge dark hands like a horse that not only respects but loves its rider, giving that extra measure that wins races or outruns doom. At the end of his solo, Cotton came back in and the Trio did one of its signature moves. Cotton blew an improvised riff on the sax, and Stubbs played it back note for note high on the bass's neck. Stubbs added a few measures, and Britton played back both their improvs, adding his own phrases. They went round-robin a few more times, and then played the whole works in unison to end the number.

Cotton acknowledged the applause, waving his hand around the stage. "We got Bobby Britton on the piano; Jack Stubbs on the bass, and I'm Cotton Breakiron. Have another drink and relax. More on the way."

Cotton headed my way as soon as he saw me, stopping to flash his smile at one table or another and high-fiving the regulars. He's one of those savvy showmen who understand that you're on stage even when you aren't 'til the crowd goes home.

He sat on the stool next to me and waved the bartender over. "Tiffany, my sweet," he said in his lilting voice, "Please bring the white boy here another beer, and tear up his tab. I'm buyin'."

"I should have ordered Dom Perignon 1957."

He laughed and pointed. "They got it right under the bar."

She brought me another Heineken and set a drink that looked like a highball in front of Cotton. I raised an eyebrow. "Ginger ale," he said.

"How many years now, Cotton?"

He fished out the maraschino cherry and bit it off the stem. "Fourteen and counting; clean and sober."

I raised my bottle and clinked his glass. "Here's to you and AA."

"I'll drink to that." He took a sip from his glass. "So what brings you uptown?"

"I need some help, man. You know Lavalle Grooms?"

"Blue Smoke?" There was a pause. "I've met him. He comes into some of the clubs."

"The cops like him for Eddie Shay's murder. I think they're wrong, and maybe I can prove it, but I need information."

"Like what?"

"I need to know about his operation, not the big machine behind him, but how he ran his show."

Cotton hesitated, looking in the mirror and thoughtfully brushing imaginary lint from his lapel with his thumb.

"When did you turn into Sam Spade?"

"When Lottie died."

"Lottie? What about her?"

"I think maybe her murder and Eddie's are connected, and Grooms is just collateral damage."

"And who you think did it?"

"Can't prove it yet, so I don't want to say, but I want his ass on the injection table."

He toyed with his drink, thinking that one over. "What I tell you, I didn't tell you, got it? Those boys don't play nice."

"I know the rules."

"Blue Smoke was strictly a wheeler dealer; ran off the phone out of his car. Customers call, he delivers."

"Like, to their houses?"

"Hell, no." Cotton snorted. "He ain't Domino's Pizza. Parking lots, fast food joints, anyplace he can roll down his window, hand out the goods to the rich folks, and run when he's done."

"No exceptions?"

"That I don't know. But I never heard different."

"Do you think you could arrange a face-to-face with him?"

"With you?" Cotton laughed. "You can't be serious, man. His people'd cut off your head and throw it in a dumpster just for laughs."

"I'm serious, Cotton. He knows something I need to know. As for Grooms, if it means the difference between a short stay for dope and maybe the death penalty for murder, I figure he'll talk to me."

Cotton thought that one over. "When you put it that way, it may sound more appealing. I'll speak to some folks and get back to you. But I have to know, Sam, and you know Blue Smoke's gonna ask, what's your stake in this?"

"Justice, Cotton."

He gave me a serious look, took a long breath then laughed. "That shit'll get you killed," and he slid off the stool, slapped my shoulder and headed back to the stage. In two minutes, the trio was back and Cotton was blowing a haunting version of "The Peacock." I finished my beer and gave him a wave as I headed out the door.

If Danny killed Eddie, how did Grooms get the ring? Was Eddie doing heavy drugs? Did Grooms make a delivery to Eddie between Lottie's visit and the murder? And why would he be in the house or at the house at all if he worked strictly out of his car? I couldn't imagine Eddie giving the ring to anyone. First, Eddie wasn't hurting for money to trade it for drugs. Second, as attached as he was to it, I'd bet Eddie would give up a finger before he'd give up the ring. If Cotton came through for me, I might get some answers.

29

The next night was the showcase party. Wendy showed up in a pleated wool skirt with a muted green plaid and a loose tan blouse under a navy blazer. She was wearing wire-rimmed glasses tonight instead of her contact lenses.

"You look like a librarian," I joked, "You can check out my book any day of the week."

"Sounds like you're long overdue." She shot back. She sat primly on the sofa, hands in her lap. "But I must say you look good tonight."

I bowed at the waist. "Thank you, Milady." I was wearing jeans and an untucked white linen shirt over a burgundy tee, neither overdressed nor under. I took my Martin D-18 from the wall, wiped it with a polishing cloth and laid it in its case.

"How old is that one?"

"About fifty years. I picked it up used when I was in school. One of my friends needed money to go to Europe, and I got a bargain. It's an oldie, but it still sounds as good as ever. Anything new from Kearny?"

"Not today. He's stalled. He's frustrated as hell and it bothers me a little to watch him twist in the wind while I sit on what I know."

"So tell him about it and maybe he'll get it right or maybe Eddie and Lottie will be two cold cases forever. Is that what you want? Besides, if you tell him now, it'll be 'what did she know and when did she know it'."

She thought about that one for a minute and nodded slowly. "That'd be it between Kearny and me. He'd never trust me again."

"Who says he trusts you now? Do you think he tells you everything he knows?"

"He holds a lot of cards close, and he uses the media like all cops do. Let a little bit out at a time, just enough to keep the public and the mayor's office off his ass. That's the secret to handling the press; give them something every day or so, just enough for a new lead line. Go to them and don't make them come looking for you. But he has kept me ahead of the *Herald* and the TV hairdos. I'd hate to lose that edge."

"Who says you will? If we're right, you hand him a killer and you both shine. If we're not, he doesn't look stupid for chasing the wrong rabbit. Ready to go?"

She stood up. "Let's not talk about Eddie, Lottie, Kearny, guns or bullets anymore tonight. Deal?"

"Deal."

As a consequence, we didn't say much as we rode across town in the van. The early evening was warm and the late sun shone like gold fire on the higher window panes as we passed through the city. Wendy thumbed through my CDs and chose Mike Stern's *Jigsaw*. The jazz came on, and she settled back in her seat and closed her eyes. I was just as happy not to talk, priming myself for the gig. I was looking forward to playing tonight, not just for the money, but for the connection.

Years ago, I was playing my regular lounge job at the Eagle's Nest Hotel, a mountaintop resort about 30 miles out of town. A high-school prom was going on in the ballroom next door, and the DJ's system was pounding bass through the wall like one of those boom cars that pull up beside you at a traffic light and make your coffee cup dance on the dashboard.

I apologized to the dozen or so folks in the lounge for the distraction and went on with my set. Kids in tuxes and gowns strolled by looking through the door. Some of them walked by again, and in pairs, they started drifting into the lounge and filling the front tables and pulling chairs close to me.

One of them requested Van Morison's "Brown Eyed Girl," and I played it. Another asked for Cat Stevens' "Moonshadow," and I played it. One by one they asked for songs from the past that they either heard on an oldies station, or on their parents' car radios growing up. It wasn't that I was terrific so much as they were fascinated by something most of them had never seen, a live performance, a man, a guitar, and music unfolding five feet away. It was *Unplugged* without the television set.

At one point I said, "You guys are missing your prom," and a kid in a black tux with spit-shined cowboy boots, a string tie and a black Stetson hat said, "This is better than any DJ." A few minutes later, the hotel manager and one of the chaperones came in and shooed the underagers out of the lounge, but for a brief, shining moment, the connection was there.

● ● ●

Two plush neighborhoods flank Hanniston. Shanks Hill is largely the enclave of the old coal families from the turn of the 20th century and their descendants. Don and Lois Siesman, being nouveau riche, lived in the Johnny-come-lately kingdom of Bell Heights.

The Seisman's lifestyle was facilitated by the marriage of two fortunes. Don's father left him an enormously successful Chevrolet dealership. Lois's father left her a pile of money garnered from his lifetime in wholesale produce. I'd never met Lois, but I'd seen Don regularly for years on television. He was one of those annoying dealers who do their own ads for new and used cars. Don's signature tag line: "Why deal? Because my deal is I-deal—for you!" He couldn't walk down any street in the tri-state area without someone calling out the slogan, accompanied by the gestures; point to your chest, point to your eye, point to the camera.

The Seismans owned the best of everything but never seemed to have the time to enjoy it because they were caught up in the forty-something yuppie quest for eternal youth. Every spare minute of their lives was spent with a tanning booth, a cosmetic dentist, a plastic surgeon, and a personal trainer.

I rang the bell and waited a full minute before ringing it again. I knew we were at the right house because of the twin wine red Denalis with vanity plates that read "GMC-HIS" and "GMC-HERS" parked side by side in the curving driveway. After the second ring, the door swung inward and Don Seisman stepped into the doorway. He was wearing a teal blue v-necked sweater and a $50,000 smile that screamed, "implants!" The sweater probably looked great draped across his shoulders with the arms crossed over his chest after a hard day at the tennis court. Gucci loafers and no socks; if he wore a hairpiece, it was a good one. He looked just like he did on television.

"Hi! Good to see you…" For a micro-second, Don's eye flicked to my guitar case to confirm the I.D. "Sam." It was obvious that Lois chose me for the evening's entertainment.

True to form, Wendy stepped forward extending her hand for a shake. "Hi! Wendy Conn from the *Sentinel*." You could almost hear the cogs click as Don's smile ratcheted up another notch. "Good to meet you. Joe Mancini said the press would be here. You can never get too much ink, right?" He swung his glance back and forth between us to include me in the fun and chuckled at his own joke. "C'mon in."

My cousin who flips houses says that the foyer of any house is one of its most crucial selling points. The foyer is the first part of the living space that a prospective buyer sees, and its impact plays a large part in negotiation and sale. The first word I thought about Don's foyer was "spectacular." The ceiling was high, the carpet was deep, and the furniture was classy. Top it off with a crystal chandelier that loomed like one of those UFOs in *Close Encounters* and threw tiny faux rainbows all over the walls and ceiling. My first thought was disco ball, but I could see Wendy was impressed despite her usual cynical affect.

Mrs. Garner, my senior English teacher, told me in high school that someday I would use all those vocabulary words I learned in Word Wealth; words like opulent, palatial, luxurious. Someday had arrived; likewise for pretentious, ostentatious, and excessive. I kept my mouth shut. That way I couldn't bite the hand that was feeding me.

Don led us through room after room of contemporary furniture and unintelligible art, all the latest and greatest to hear him tell it. I felt like Nick Carraway walking through Gatsby's mansion, but for all its luster, the place was too new to have class. It was raw money.

"We decided to put you in here," he led us into a game room almost as big as my whole apartment. A pool table and a wet bar dominated one end of the room and couches and recliners were grouped at the other. A fire was blazing in the fireplace and a stool had been set up for me to one side of the hearth opposite a huge flat screen TV set. A football game flashed across its face, the sound muted. The chairs and sofas were grouped to focus on the stool. I suspected that any other time they'd face the television. "Will this be okay?"

I nodded. The room had a lower ceiling than the others and acoustics wouldn't be a problem. I figured the Martin would sound pretty good. "Yeah, this will work. I may move the stool around a little to find the sweet spot, but I won't be able to do that until the guests are in their seats." I set down my guitar and opened the case to let thermodynamics do its work. Like most fine old instruments, my Martin is sensitive to climate. No point in tuning it until it reached room temperature. The heat from the fireplace wouldn't be a problem if I kept myself turned the right direction.

Don was one of those people uncomfortable with silence that lasts longer than three seconds, and he jumped in to fill the empty spaces. "Yeah, we spend most of our time at home in here." He chuckled, "Lois hates to ruffle the carpets in the other rooms." I had visions of velvet ropes hanging across doorways like the ones you see in historical houses. "She works hard to make the place look great."

He was fishing for a compliment, so Wendy took the bait. "The house is marvelous. Everything is so fresh." Don beamed. I had a feeling that he'd quote Wendy for the next decade to anyone who would listen. "How about a drink?" At the bar, the caterer's bartender was setting up shop. I had a Corona and Wendy had a frozen margarita that she pronounced "excellent" when prompted by Don.

"Come on out to the deck." Don led us through patio doors to a redwood deck the size of Rhode Island. At one end, caterers were fussing over a table full of everything. At the other end, umbrella tables and comfortable patio furniture sat at odd angles, most of it facing the back yard where an in-ground pool glowed like an aquamarine in the twilight. I had a feeling Don was waiting for me to ask him how much it all cost, so I didn't.

"You guys relax. I have a few details to take care of, but I'll be right back." He sauntered off, stopping to give some directions to the caterers, accompanied by lots of gestures and finger pointing. The caterers shrugged, picked up a table of canapés and moved it five feet closer to the doorway. They were accustomed to dealing with the Dons of the world and took it in stride. I envied them that.

Wendy broke the silence. "What are you thinking, Sam?"

"That maybe I could have enjoyed all this if things went a different way, but would I really want it? I guess I've lived the way I do for so long this just seems unnatural."

"Aberrant."

"Weird."

"Grotesque."

"Surreal."

"Kafkaesque."

I laughed. "You win. I can't top that one." I leaned back in my chair and took another long look over the backyard. "My dad had it right. He always said, 'You live in your own head. All you really need is food, clothing, and a safe place to sleep.' That and a La-Z-Boy recliner."

"He said that?"

"I added the recliner because he wouldn't admit it."

"Sounds like a wise man."

"Yeah, too bad I didn't inherit any of that wisdom; I turned out to be more of a wise guy."

Wendy smiled. "You're wiser than you think, Sam. As a matter of fact you're the wisest guy I've been around for a long time."

At that moment, Lois Seisman burst through the patio doors in a tornado of last minute attention to detail. Lois was dressed in the kind of

"All you really need is food, clothing, and a safe place to sleep."

outfit that is calculated to look eclectic; a peasant blouse over jeans that flattered her lower half, mid-heel clogs and an armful of jangling bracelets: Gypsy manqué. She was in mid-sentence, telling one of the caterers about the kebabs when she spotted us and scurried over.

Her tan matched Don's and so did her teeth. Words tumbled from her like water gushing from a drainpipe. "Hi! I'm Lois Seisman, Sam. And you must be Wendy Conn. It's great to have you both here. We're all looking forward to tonight. We thought about having it out here on the deck, but we were afraid of the weather. Well, I've got to get a few things ready, so enjoy yourselves. The guests will be here soon." And she was gone. "Well, it's finally happened," I said.

"What?"

"I've finally met someone who can talk as well inhaling as she can exhaling. The things I do for money."

• • •

The guests arrived in ones and twos, and soon the game room was buzzing with talk, laughter, and the crack of balls on the pool table. Lois took me by the elbow from person to person to introduce me to everyone. She compensated for my lack of schmoozing skills with an overdose of her own. By eight-thirty, Lois gave me the name and pedigree of every person in the room but the bartender.

Don bellowed over the chatter, "Okay, everybody, show time!" He shouted through the patio doors to some people on the deck. "Everybody inside!" A handful of guests trooped in with their drinks as everyone took a seat. The caterers provided some extra folding chairs that looked more comfortable than the lounger in my living room.

Lois took over, beaming radiantly. "Most of you have met Sam Dunne already this evening." She gestured toward me to a spatter of applause. "He is a long-time performer and recording artist, and a former member of Gin Sing, and right now he's going to make our evening special." To her credit, she shut off the football game.

I took my seat on the stool and the chatter subsided. I tuned a few minutes earlier but checked it anyway. The G string was a little flat—always the G. I launched into "Lady Will You Stay" and a few faces registered recognition. The song had hit locally and was slated for a Travis Daye LP early next spring. It was a good song for an opener because the extended instrumental chorus at the start let me listen to the sound of the guitar and feel out the acoustics of the room before I started to sing.

"Lady, will you stay, 'til I put my guitar away, or would you fade like the final chords of my last melody?" The lyric tells the story of a singer-songwriter wooing a woman with his music and is usually a favorite with audiences. I scanned the room as I sang and saw that by the end of the second verse most of the guests were locked onto the song. One or two were singing with me under their breath. By the time I reached the end of the last verse, "My guitar is in its case; won't you please come and take its place," I pretty much had them, the women for sure.

The song ended to enthusiastic applause. I looked to Wendy, who gave me a smile and a thumbs-up. "This song is from my upcoming CD *Gloves Off*." I always mentioned an upcoming CD as part of my patter. It kept people interested and committed me to the next big thing. I played a soft rocker, "Smiling With Your Eyes" next, watching for crowd response. They liked it well enough, but it was time to shift gears.

"Here's one from my first CD, *Three Rounds*." I kicked up the opening of "Top Thirteen," a hard-line acoustic blues song and people's heads started to bob and weave to the rhythm. "Don't think 'cause you're a younger man that makes you a better lover. Them women ain't gonna read your book once I rip off the cover." Somewhere in the middle of the solo, someone started clapping in time and a few others picked it up. One of the women stood up and started doing a slow twisty dance, hands over her head and I let the solo run for another round before I sang the last verse. The applause was louder now.

"If any of you has a favorite song of mine, I'll be happy to do it for you."

Lois stood and turned so that she was aimed obliquely at me and at the guests at the same time. "Actually, we were hoping . . ."

Red Flag. I cocked my head in her direction. She was waiting for me to take the bait and ask "for what?" I disappointed her.

Lois had the same aversion to silence as did her husband. "We were hoping that you might spend some time telling us about Eddie." That lit my fuse. She went on, "And since we're lucky enough to have Wendy Conn with us tonight as well, maybe she can give us an inside look at the murder investigation."

I looked out at the crowd. They were all leaning in, attentive, eyes glistening in anticipation at this sudden unexpected extra. That was why the Seismans asked for me specifically, to amuse their friends by pandering to their morbid curiosity. I shot a look at Wendy. She shrugged and shook her head. She was as blindsided by this as I was.

I gave Lois a hard glare that burned into her eyeballs until she turned away. Everyone in the room was staring at me. "That's not why I'm here," I said through my teeth. I scanned the room. "Is that why all of you came?" No response. To Lois, I said, "Did you clear this with Joe?" Her mouth opened and moved a few times but nothing came out.

"You want to know about Eddie Shay? I'll tell you about Eddie. He didn't give a damn for creatures like you. I can't speak for Wendy, but I'm not going to sit here and tell a flock of vultures some campfire stories about him. He's dead, murdered, and you're sick, all of you! The whole gang of you put together isn't good enough to kiss his ass—or mine. I'm out of here."

I stood and the stool fell over behind me, clattering on the hearth. I unstrapped my guitar and put it in the case, the latches snapping shut like fire crackers in the stunned silence. Lois turned to Don, her hands palm up in a gesture of helplessness. He bulled forward and confronted me as I stood up, guitar case in hand.

"These people have paid good money hear you." I picked up my canvas carry bag and dumped thirty or so of my CDs on the floor. I said to the room at large. "Please accept these CDs in lieu of a refund."

I looked to Wendy. She stood up to leave with me. Don grabbed my right arm head on with his left hand just above the elbow. His fingers dug into my bicep. It's amazing how easily those friendly teeth turn into fangs. "Who do you think you are? You aren't walking out on us."

My right forearm shot out and over his hand, catching it in the crook of my elbow and bending his hand backward to a painful angle. He dropped to one knee, grunting in pain. At the least, I'd sprained his wrist. I said quietly, "Keep your hands to yourself, unless you want your wife and friends to watch you get your ass kicked." As I let him go two of his bigger pals started forward flexing their beer muscles. I turned obliquely toward them, set down my guitar and planted my feet at right angles, one behind the other for stability. I flexed my hands. We stared at each other for a long breath, and suddenly, Don decided to forget the whole thing. He stood up. "Screw him. Let him go. He's a loser anyway." Maybe he and Lois didn't want blood on the carpet.

On the way down the driveway, I was ready to heave a good sized ficus in a five-gallon terra cotta pot onto the hood of one of the matched Denalis but couldn't make up my mind which one I wanted to trash more, GMC-HIS or GMC-HERS .

30

Neither of us said anything for a few minutes. My anger cooled to a slow burn by the time we hit uptown. "Sorry you had to be a part of that," I said.

"Don't apologize. It's never wrong to be true to yourself. Joe had no right to let that happen."

"But he did. And it did. He always played square with me up to now but this was over the line. I could have sucked it up and played the game, but I'd feel like a hooker selling out that way."

"Maybe you can work it out between you. Give it a chance. Things always look better in the morning."

"Maybe so. Hey, the night's young. Go for a drink? Harrigan's is close. So is The Brass Duck."

"Or we could just go to my place," she said, looking out her window. "Take a left two blocks up onto Montrose."

I almost asked her how she'd get her car, but I caught myself just in time.

Wendy lived in a one-story cottage-style house with a separate garage and a bathmat of a lawn. It was brick to the waist and siding to the peak with dark shutters. The street light at the curb cast the shadow of two good sized trees over a small front porch. It would be cool and shady in the summer, but tonight the autumn leaves blocked the street lights.

I parked in the driveway and followed her across the yard. Her skirt swung side to side and her heels clicked on the porch steps. She fished in her bag for her keys. "Someday I'll find time to change the bulb in the porch light and life will be easier."

"Yeah, you never know who might sneak up behind you in the dark."

She turned and in the dim light I could see her smile for the first time without looking like a shark. "On second thought, maybe I'll leave it alone."

Inside, the house was small and tidy, very little clutter and very little dust. The living room had a tan leather love seat and matching sofa. The rugs looked Southwestern, Mexican or Indian; I couldn't tell you for sure. I'm no decorator. Poster-sized framed photos of desert scenes hung on the walls. In one corner a red conical fireplace poked its chimney through the ceiling. A Bose sat on an end table. No TV.

"This room looks comfortable."

"It is. Why don't you build a fire while I get us something to drink. You want a beer?"

"Your house, your choice; surprise me. I'll have whatever you do." She went to the kitchen and I crouched by the fireplace and balled up some newspaper.

I heard glasses clink and her voice from the next room. "Don't forget to open the flue, or this will be a short evening."

I turned the wire-twist handle and heard the metal flap move in the stovepipe. I figured half would do it. Soon the fire was laid and I lit a long match on the striker. In a minute, a warm yellow glow filled the room. I sank into the sofa and leaned my head against the high cushioned back. I closed my eyes for a second and something landed in my lap.

A big black cat stood on my thighs, its eyes glowing in the firelight. It dropped and curled up just below my belt buckle. Wendy appeared in the doorway. "That's Cassandra. She likes you. That's a good sign." I scratched the cat behind its ears and it purred like a vibrator. Wendy handed me a stemmed glass. "I hope you like wine. This is a nice chardonnay."

She sat on the love seat, tucking her legs under her skirt, playing it cautious and keeping her distance, I guess. I sipped the wine and almost regretted not asking for a beer. "Forgive me if I fall asleep. This couch is too comfortable."

"Like Baby Bear's bed, it's just right."

"Like this house," I said, eyes wandering around. "It suits you."

"It's about the right size, just like your apartment."

"Did you take the pictures?" I gestured around the room with my glass.

She nodded. "I took those when I worked for a paper in Tucson. I miss the desert."

"Lonely place, huh?"

"What?" She tilted her head, puzzled.

"Lonely place. All that space and no people." I pointed to a sprawling vista of sand and saguaro. "The scenery's beautiful, but there are no people in your pictures."

She didn't speak for a minute. She held her glass up to watch the flames dance through the wine. "Gets to be a way of life after a while. You've been married, right Sam?"

"Once. Almost twice."

"Yeah, I heard you had an 'Ex' rating from one of the women at the office."

"Which one?"

"How many did you date?"

I laughed. "One too many, I guess. And you?"

"Once, when I was out west. It lasted two years, and I got the ultimatum from Rob: divorce my career or he'd divorce me."

"Sounds familiar. My friend Danny Workman always said a man can't be a good guitar player and a good husband at the same time. I guess I'm living proof. I can't blame Cheryl. The night she left, she said. 'If it was another woman, I'd at least know how to compete, but how do I compete with a guitar?'"

Wendy shook her head. "Just like "Dead Man's Melody,' there are days when I think most of us live one day too many, but we never know which one 'til it's too late."

"Cheryl took a walk on me eight years ago. How long have you been divorced?"

"I'm not. Four years ago I was doing a series on a Mexican drug cartel using children as mules. They shot up my car. I caught one in the leg and Rob caught one in the head. I'm a widow. That's why I left Tucson after I finished the series; not because I was afraid of the bad guys, but because I couldn't stand the reminders on every street corner."

So much for breezy conversation. She set her glass down and moved over beside me. Almost on cue, Cassandra leaped from my lap and stalked out of the room. Wendy put her arms around my neck and pulled my face to hers, forehead to forehead. "I like you, Sam. I like you a lot, but I'm afraid."

"Afraid of what?"

"Of letting myself want something again, and maybe even getting it and then losing it."

I took her face in my hands and looked into her eyes. I tilted her chin and kissed her lightly on the mouth. She grabbed the back of my head with both hands and kissed me back; not exactly Wendy and Razor, but close enough.

She leaned back on the sofa pulling me onto her and all the time kissing me hard, gnawing at my lower lip, panting hot in my ear. I unbuttoned her blouse and leaned in to kiss the tops of her breasts. She wrapped her hands around the back of my head and crushed my face between them. I ran my hand up her thigh and squeezed her hip. She wrapped a leg around mine.

The phone rang in the next room.

"Dammit," Wendy hissed. It rang again. She ignored it. It rang again. She pushed away and padded to the next room. "The paper's on caller I.D." It rang again. "I better take it."

I could hear her pick up. "Hello?" Irritation bristled in her voice. "Yeah, Kurt. Yeah, I know my cell is off. I'm off. Where? Why can't Smith cover it? He's on tonight, isn't he?" An exasperated sigh. "All right, but you and he both owe me big time." She hung up a little too hard and in a second she came back and stood in the living room doorway. "God, I'm sorry, Sam, but a body just turned up in Headley Park and I have to cover it. Guess you can see now why I'm single. Can you take me to my car?"

I thought about taking her straight to the park instead but figured that could get complicated, especially if Kearny took the call for homicide. "No problem; rain checks are redeemable."

She smiled sadly. "Be ready in a minute." She dashed back to her bedroom to change and I carried the wine glasses to the kitchen. Cassandra watched me from her basket-bed as I rinsed them in the sink and set them upside down on the drain board. Wendy came back in a minute, as promised, in jeans and a sweater. One more minute and we were out the door and in the van.

When we got to my place, she leaned across the console and kissed me gently. "Thanks for understanding, Sam." She ran to her car, and with a flash of taillights, she was gone. The rest of that night I was haunted by thoughts of a chance missed and an image from Wendy's kitchen: a half-round breakfast table against the wall opposite the sink and beside it, a single café chair.

32

The next morning, my cell phone rang. It was Joe. I debated letting it go to voice mail but took the call instead. "Hello, Joe."

"Sam, I want you to know I had nothing to do with that stunt the Seismans pulled on you last night. I would never agree something like that."

"This is going to be quick today, because I'm still steamed about it. We go back a long time, Joe, and you've never lied to me. For that I'm giving you the benefit of the doubt. Don't ever let something like that happen again."

"Fair enough, but I'll tell you something too. You can't go around roughing up the people who hire you. I'm guessing I won't land you a gig like that one again in your lifetime, and that hurts my wallet as much as it hurts yours. Grow some self-control, will you?"

As I hung up, it occurred to me that if the deal with Sunsong weren't in the works, Joe would have written me off without blinking. I love leverage.

• • •

Later that day I called both of the numbers Danny scrawled on the napkin at the Avalanche. Both calls went to voice mail, maybe because he didn't recognize my number, or maybe because he was too stoned to answer it. "Danny, it's Sam Dunne. Call me." I didn't bother leaving a number; he'd get it from his Caller I.D.

Danny rang back in three minutes.

"Yeah?"

"It's Danny, Sam. I guess you made up your mind?"

"Like you said, the deal has promise, but I'm letting Joe Mancini handle negotiations with the suits."

He didn't say anything and I let the silence build like a cold snowfall. Make him break it. This gambit was supposed to lull him, but I couldn't help myself. I didn't say a word. Finally he broke. "I wish you would have talked it over with me first."

"I did a couple of nights ago, remember?"

"Man, I'm trying to help you. Why are you so goddammed hostile?"

"Do you pet the dog that bit your hand?" Another long pause. "Hey, just messin' with you dude." I laughed.

He believed me because he wanted to. "Oh, man. You had me goin.'" He laughed too, but nervously.

"So, once the ink's dry and the champagne corks pop, we can start making music."

"Yeah. Listen, can you get those songs of yours to me?"

"I can e-mail you the files. Do you use Finale?"

"Nah. I never got into the computers much. Eddie handled all that stuff."

"Well, my demos are a little rough. Give me a day and I'll clean them up and get them to you."

"Or you could just come over and play them for me yourself. How about tonight?"

"I had some plans. Let me make a few calls and see if I can get out of them."

He laughed a little less nervously. "Bring her with you."

"And have you snake her right out from under me? I'm not that dumb, Danny."

He laughed again. "Or come afterward. We never close."

"I'll call you back."

I had to think this one through very carefully. As soon as he thought I was in, Danny was back to angling. He wanted to hear my songs and try to get a hand in them before the deal was set. He didn't want any song on the LP that didn't have his name on it. A useful piece of information: Danny didn't read music, so he never learned to use Finale, and he wouldn't have known how to find the lead sheet for "You and Me" on Eddie's computer. He may have destroyed the copyright form and a printed lead sheet, the ashes in the fireplace, but I still had proof Danny didn't know about that he stole the song.

I was leery about going to Danny's house, but if I went, his ego wouldn't let me leave before he showed off every inch of the place. I could take a good look at the layout and grease my wheels for later. And if I took Wendy.... I grabbed my phone and punched in her number.

"Sam. I can only talk for a minute; I'm up against a deadline."

"Stop the presses." I laughed. "Does anybody ever really say that?"

"Not in my lifetime."

"So what is it today? Somebody knock off an armored car? Big drug bust?"

She sighed. "Nothing exciting, just cat and dog stuff; the usual assaults, rapes, shootings, stick-ups—life in the big city. What's up?"

"If you have plans for tonight, cancel them. You're going with me to visit Danny Barton."

A pause. "O-ka-a-y. How did this happen?"

"Come by around eight and I'll fill you in. Come in costume."

"As what?"

"Irresistible."

That earned me another pause. "I see, I think. Shiner?"

"*Vidae, cogito.* My Latin's a little flaky, but you get the idea."

"Eight. The adventure continues. Now shut up and hang up so I can get some work done."

Danny could never resist trying to take any woman away from any man, including Eddie and me. It became a running joke between us. He was the perpetual side three of the eternal triangle. If I read Danny right, he'd run after Wendy like a dog on a rabbit, just because he thought she was mine. It's funny how things play out; Wendy after me for a story; me after Danny for justice; Danny after her for his ego. Not exactly the eternal triangle, more like an infernal one.

Two of the three songs I wanted to pitch, "One Finger in Ten" and "Watchin' You Walk" were already copyrighted but I hadn't circulated them to labels and artists yet. If I was going to play them for Danny, all three had to be sewn up legally for my protection. If I worked fast, I could prepare a lead sheet for the third song, "Hourglass" and file the copyright online this afternoon. I could have used three lesser songs, but my numbers, music and lyrics were gold to Danny's tin and I wanted to rub his nose in it. Yeah, I was being petty—so what?

33

I called Danny back late in the afternoon. He took the call on the first ring this time. "Yeah, Sam?" I hate Caller I. D. It's too much like a major-domo announcing arrivals at a formal dinner before they walk into the room. No surprises.

"Danny." I did my best to sound congenial although I wanted to reach through the phone and rip out his throat. I managed to do a passable job.

"What's the word?" Compared to earlier today, his tone seemed almost carefree. I suspected he was already two or three drinks into the celebration, or maybe two or three joints. He was too mellow for it to be coke.

"I'll come tonight."

"Outstanding."

I asked for his address although I already knew it. I drove by the day before to see the place in daylight.

"213 Haller Drive."

"Where's Haller?"

"Northside. You cross the Memorial Bridge and take..." and he rambled through a set of directions full of short cuts and side streets that would confuse a homing pigeon.

"Tell you what; I'll look it up on MapQuest and print it out. You know me; I could get lost between my kitchen and living room. Eight-thirty okay?"

"Sure. You'll have to excuse the looks of the place." He laughed, almost a giggle. "It's the maid's year off." He giggled again at his own joke. "Later."

"Yeah, Danny, later." I shut my phone thinking, it's a lot later than you know.

• • •

Wendy was early as usual. She wore a pleated navy blue skirt and a plain white silk blouse, elegant in its simplicity.

"'Whenas in silks my Julia goes, then, then methinks how sweetly flows that liquefaction of her clothes. Next, when I cast mine eyes, and see that brave vibration each way free, O how that glittering taketh me!'"

She gave me a skeptical smile and looked at me from the corner of her eye. "Bet you say that to all the girls."

I shrugged, palms up. "Worked for Robert Herrick." I started back to the bedroom.

"Where are you going?"

I looked down at my chinos and sweater. "To put on something with a little more class." I said over my shoulder, "There's some chardonnay in the fridge. Help yourself." Yeah, I bought it that afternoon. No harm in trying.

My bedroom closet is packed as tight as my bookshelves and on the rare occasions when I wear one of my suits, I usually have to hang it in the bathroom and run the shower for ten minutes to steam out the wrinkles. Of the four, my grey suit was in the best shape. I dug a black linen shirt out of the mass and tried it under the coat. Not bad. I opted out of a tie and left my collar open. For my money, anybody who buttons his shirt to the neck without a tie or unbuttons it to his navel looks like a horse's ass.

Wendy sat on the sofa drinking from a highball glass. She was leafing through *The Oxford Anthology of English Verse*. "Couldn't find your stemware," she said.

"That's because I haven't found it yet myself."

"Robert Herrick's poetry is as hedonistic as your lyrics: 'Gather ye rosebuds, while ye may, Old Time is still a-flying: and this same flower that smiles to-day to-morrow will be dying.' Grab it while you can. Things haven't changed much in four hundred years, have they?"

"The poets were the rock stars of their day."

"Speaking of rock stars, what's tonight's agenda?"

I laid out my plan to use the visit to case Danny's house and to introduce them to promote the interview. "He doesn't know you're coming, so you'll be a pleasant surprise. There's another reason I want you along, too. I'm going to play some new songs for Danny. I figure he'll have a recorder running someplace, and I need a credible witness that I auditioned these songs for him on this date. I don't want him telling the label he and I wrote them together."

"Anything else I need to know? I keep thinking about your stunt with the pictures and the copyright form. Anything else you're not telling me?"

"No. That's it. Just be your charming self and act fascinated with everything Danny says."

"In other words, become Donna Fields. I feel like a character from *Hustle*. Ever see the show?"

"Robert Vaughn and his team of Brit con artists? Yeah, I loved it."

She finished her wine and set the glass on the coffee table. "Me too, but that was TV; this is real. You think this guy's a murderer, Sam, right?" I nodded. "I'll do a lot for a story, but I don't want to end up in a drawer in the File Room."

34

We took the van to Danny's house. Wendy's degree of calm was impressive. I know she stared down mob guys and thugs every day and played in the same sandbox with some really bad people, but a quiet dinner one-one-one across the table from a killer would be working without a net. Maybe she played the tough gal for so long that her mask became her face, or maybe she really was that tough. Either way, I admired her cool. She cranked her seat back and closed her eyes, hands open in her lap.

"You said Eddie's house was pretty much in the open, no security cameras, no fences."

"I don't think I said that; maybe Kearny told you."

She let that one slide. "How about Danny's?"

"I drove past it in the daytime and didn't see anything obvious. As for the inside, that's what tonight is about."

"I thought celebrities all lived behind ten-foot walls with broken glass embedded in the tops."

"There's a hierarchy in stardom; Gin Sing was big news years ago, but not anymore, and I don't think Danny has to worry about paparazzi or stalkers. Old jocks have more trouble than old rockers. Some fan might bother him for an autograph in the middle of a restaurant or want to take a picture with him once in a while, but that's as far as it goes now. Take him out of Hanniston and I doubt anybody would even recognize him. And if he told them his name, they'd say, 'Who?' And he'd say, 'No, Gin Sing.'"

She groaned at my joke. "Don't quit your day job, Sam."

I went on. "Eddie and Danny were lucky they made enough money all along that they didn't end up selling life insurance or real estate like some of yesteryear's idols. But neither of them has to live with bodyguards and electric fences."

"So it's like the *Sesame Street* song, 'The rock star is a person in your neighborhood.'"

"You got it. He buys cigarettes at the 7-Eleven and rolls his garbage cans to the curb every Monday like the rest of us these days, but I'm sure he wishes otherwise. You can't call him a has-been because Gin Sing is still current, but he's slipping in that direction."

"Must hurt his ego, drifting into anonymity, but would he kill people to stop it?"

"In the end you can never stop it, but maybe he thinks he can hold it off just a little bit longer."

In the course of a few minutes, the drive moved us from four lanes and interchanges to two lanes lined with strip malls and store fronts and finally to quiet streets with little traffic. Danny's place was an old two story brick house with dormers and gables in a neighborhood full of them set back from the tree lined street by deep lawns. The neighborhood spoke of bygone days when coal was king in Pennsylvania, and money was as plentiful as the coal. When we pulled into the driveway, we saw lights blazing from every room on the ground floor and most of the rooms on the second.

"Looks like a party," Wendy said, reaching for the door handle.

"Wait." I held out my hand. A pair of keys dangled from a key ring. "Take these."

"Your car keys? Planning on getting too drunk to drive?"

"Just playing it safe; these are spares. I don't expect any problems, but if something goes wrong, I want you to get out and get help."

She put the key ring in her purse and climbed out of the van. "So many lights; if it's not a party, he's afraid of the dark."

The bass of a loud stereo thumped through the walls and rolled over the lawn. "I bet the neighbors love him." Although the house was bright on the inside, the wide covered porch was dark. My foot brushed a beer can that fell over with a clank and noisily rolled away; one more thing to watch out for when I came back. I didn't see a button for a doorbell, so I knocked. Then I pounded. Then I waited for a break in the music and pounded harder.

In a minute, a short blonde woman answered the door. She wore a bottle green dress too short for her heavy legs and too tight for her figure. The corners of her eyes radiated lines like fine cracks in china. Everything about her said "hooker," but I reserved judgment.

"Hi, you must be Sam. I'm Doris. Come on in." She looked past me and saw Wendy and her welcoming smile tightened a little. Thinking I was coming alone, maybe Danny arranged for her to brighten my evening. Wendy and I stepped into the hallway and I immediately smelled the burnt pork chop odor of reefer.

The contrast between Eddie's house and Danny's was evident from the foyer onward. Eddie's house was outfitted with a certain amount of hip taste, even if it wasn't his own, and while it was lived in, it was well kept. Danny's looked like an older couple's home trashed by college-age grandkids and their pals. It occurred to me that he rented the place furnished and exhibited an insouciant disregard for its preservation.

An amplifier and mic stand with a fine film of dust stood to the left inside the door, set down and forgotten coming home from a late-night gig. The hall table was piled with unopened mail and magazines.

"Danny's in the living room," said Doris over her shoulder. "This way."

We followed her into a high-ceilinged room that was big enough that it shouldn't have looked cluttered, but the size and amount of its furniture made it so. The room was full of wing-backed chairs and sofas from a bygone era, two different sets of them, as if the second set were dragged in from the parlor next door. They were arranged so that the focus of the room was the enormous flat screen TV that hung like a mini Jumbotron on one wall. The coffee table was littered with ashtrays, beer cans and glasses. A baggie full of grass and a pipe lay on one of the end tables.

Danny was sprawled on one of the couches head to head with a red-haired woman dressed like Doris. One shirt tail was out over his jeans and the waistband button was undone. They were laughing like fools at some private joke.

Nearby, other people, eight or ten of them in twos and alone, drank, smoked, and generally misbehaved. I recognized two of the men from Sunsong; one was from P.R. and I couldn't place the other. The rest of Danny's guests were twenty-somethings, a younger crowd who seemed perfectly comfortable with Danny, as if he were the favorite bachelor uncle who bought beer for his underage nieces and nephews and let them borrow his living room for some heavy petting.

I turned to the television and was startled to see my face on the screen.

It was a video of an old Gin Sing show. The song was "Thinkin' Pink." I went into a solo and my guitar screamed through the stack of amps behind me. My long cascade of notes led back to the vocal, and the frame froze onscreen. The sudden silence was unsettling.

"Old times, Sambo!" Danny boomed with the lilt in his voice that people get when they're on the verge of one drink too many. He knew I always hated his pet nickname for me, but maybe he forgot. He pushed himself up from the sofa. "Good times!" He crossed the room tucking in his shirt and put an arm around my shoulders. With his glasses off, the hollows around his eyes looked darker and the lines deeper than they did on *Jumpstart*. Score one for the makeup artists.

"Everybody, this is the real, honest-to-goodness Sam Dunne, guitar player extraordinaire and songwriter to the stars." Danny's friends waved and nodded. Danny turned to Wendy, seeing her for the first time. "And the lady?"

"The real honest-to-goodness Wendy Conn," she said when I didn't speak fast enough. She stepped forward and shook Danny's hand. "Mild-mannered reporter for a daily metropolitan newspaper. Pleased to meet you." The irony was lost on Danny, but I laughed in spite of myself.

If Wendy's brass took Danny by surprise, he recovered quickly. "Come on in, sit down, have a drink. We were just watching the glory days."

He aimed the remote at the DVR and the video resumed. So did the noise level. He thumbed the mute button and turned Eddie's vocal into a silent movie. It's that easy, to shut somebody off, I thought, just push a button—or pull a trigger.

"Ladies and gentlemen, tonight we're here to celebrate a reunion, Sam and me. Gin Sing lives!" To a chorus of "Yeah!" and "All right!" He grabbed a bottle of Jack Daniels from the coffee table and held it by the neck, raising it in a toast. "To you, Sam. To us." He took a long pull from the bottle and handed it to me.

"And to Eddie." It took some self-control, but I didn't wipe the bottle on my sleeve. I tipped it up and took enough into my mouth to make my breath convincing. Then I let it flow back into the bottle when I let it down. I had to play the game, but this was no night to get drunk.

The conversation buzzed up again and Danny leaned in to speak in my ear. "I heard from Jack Paine at Sunsong a little while ago." The affected slur was gone. "I probably shouldn't be telling you, Sam, but they're gung-ho to get you on board. They said your boy Joe is twisting them pretty hard, but they think it'll be a done deal by the end of the week." He stepped back

I...was startled to see my face on the screen.

and leveled his gaze at me. Without his tinted glasses, I could see that although his eyes were glassy from the booze and red from the grass, that he was a long way from incoherent or careless. He turned away from me and said at a higher volume, "So, let's celebrate!" He thumbed the remote and Gin Sing blared from the home theater system.

I got a beer for Wendy and one for myself from an ice chest in the corner and we sat on one of the sofas. She watched the video for a few minutes then turned to me and said, "You looked angry then."

"I was." I sat back and watched as the onscreen Sam Dunne scowled, attacking the guitar as if he wanted to rake its strings from the neck. I was leaner then, but not much. My hair was longer, my hairline was closer to my eyebrows, and I was clean shaven. The auto accident that left scars under my lower lip and behind my chin hadn't happened yet, and I didn't need the beard to hide them.

"Why were you angry?"

"Because I knew I'd always be a second-stringer to those two, no matter how well I played."

The camera switched to Danny and his friends howled. "Look at that shirt! Polyester City! I can't believe you wore shit like that!" one of them yelled, pointing to the screen.

Danny put on an air of fake indignation. "Hey! Remember whose booze you're drinking. No dissing the host, dude. I'll have you know that shirt's upstairs right now hanging in the closet. I'm saving it for the Rock'n'Roll Hall of Fame." More howls of laughter.

The video ran for a few more songs and when it ended, Danny pushed a few more buttons, and some newer Gin Sing poured out of the speakers. Danny and his girl friend *du soir*, whose name was Patrice—"just call me Treecie…" plopped down on the sofa next to ours. Danny shouted over the music, "So, Sam, glad to get back in the saddle?"

"Ain't there yet." I smiled. "I'll let you know when the ink's dry."

"Like I told you, Sam, it's a done deal."

Wendy perked up. "Oh, Sam, that's great!" She moved to the edge of her seat to talk around me to Danny. "He was so worried that things wouldn't work out. Did you have a lot to do with the decision?" Wendy could talk to anybody in a room full of people and make him feel as if he were the only person there.

"I told them it was Sambo or nobody." He punctuated the sentence with a nod.

"I want to hear all about it," she said. "Maybe I could do a feature on it for the paper, if you'd be nice enough to give me an interview." She smiled at him, stopping just short of batting her eyelashes.

I thought maybe she moved too fast, but Danny beamed. "Sure thing. We can set that up."

I moved forward between them. "So, Danny, this is a nice crib, lots of space. How about a tour?"

"Sure. Just don't look too close. I'm not the tidiest person on the planet." He patted Treecie on the cheek and said, "Be back in a little bit," then to us, "This way folks."

The ground floor was four big rooms; the living room, a front room across the hallway, a dining room and the kitchen. The front room had almost no furniture, apparently the source of the extras in the living room. The dining room had an old heavy table with ball and claw feet and carved chairs. The table was littered with dirty plates and institutional-sized takeout containers from a Tex-Mex restaurant, and of course a line of empty Coors cans along one edge of the table as if they were standing guard over the wreckage of dinner.

The kitchen was a longer room than the others spanning most of the back of the house. It opened at one end into a walk-in pantry with more empty shelves than full ones. A doorway led to a mud room and past it, another into the back yard. The back door was steel and had three small eye-level panes of glass. I noted that the lock was keyed from both sides but there were no extra deadbolts or other security items. The door opened inward, right to left, and the keypad was at shoulder level to the right of the doorjamb.

I peered through the glass panes in the door. "You have a nice big yard out front," I said. "How about the back?"

He reached past me and flipped a light switch. The porch light came on. It dimly lit a shorter back yard than the front. A flagstone walk led to the one-car garage on the alley. "Not as big as the front, but I'm not much of an outdoor person anyway."

He turned away and I tried the other switch on the plate. An overhead light came on in the mud room. Outside, a neighbor's dog, a big golden Labrador, meandered across the yard, stopping to take a crap in the grass. No flood lights came on. Good news: no burglar lights on the backyard. Bad news: no convenient set of keys hanging from a hook by the door.

I saw no signs of a dog in the downstairs; no dish full of water, no bag of kibble in the pantry, and no pet toys lying around. I heard no barking outside at another dog invading the home turf. More good news. But I wasn't surprised. A dog would mean responsibility, something Danny avoided at all cost.

He was regaling Wendy with some anecdote about the old refrigerator and its contents. Danny steered her around by the elbow to point out something by the stove. Of all the places you could touch somebody, the shoulder, the hand, the waist, the knee, the ass for that matter, the elbow seems the most neutral, but Danny made even that innocuous gesture seem sleazy. Wendy was hip to Danny's act, but watching her fawn over him still set my teeth on edge. Maybe I was a little bit jealous, or maybe it reminded me of too many bygone times and bygone girls who fell for Danny's charm at my expense.

Four bedrooms and a bathroom filled the upstairs space. Three of the bedrooms formed an ell around the bath, linked to each other by interconnecting doors. The bathroom floor was done in those little black and white hexagonal tiles you remember from bus station and restaurant rest rooms when you were a kid. The bathtub was original equipment, a free standing ball-and-claw job deep enough to drown in.

"Love the tub," Wendy said. "And the sink. I love those old X faucet handles."

"Honey, everything in this place is rated X," Danny said with a leer.

If I'd said that an hour ago at my place, I'd've gotten an eye roll and a groan, maybe a shot in the ribs. Danny got a sidewise smile and a sultry look from half-closed eyes. Wendy knew how to play.

Two of the bedrooms featured unmade beds and the litter of casual sex. The third was filled with guitars, amplifiers, speakers and other gear. "This is the jam room," Danny said.

"Where's the booth?" My eyes swept the room and found none of the home studio essentials.

"No booth," he quipped. "You can't record in here. The sound in this place is lousy, and my landlord would sue me if I knocked out a wall or two. Besides, it makes no sense to invest a lot of cash in a place I don't own. I did all the major recording at Sunsong and the preliminary stuff at Eddie's."

Wendy cut in. "Now that he's gone, where will you guys do your thing?"

Danny shrugged. "We haven't gotten that far yet."

While Wendy kept his attention, I feigned interest in some of the guitars, moving around the room. I lifted an old Gibson Hummingbird from its stand and strummed it, my back to them and my eyes taking in every detail. On a table in a back corner of the room I saw a familiar black box. A Rec-Tech was propped on edge against the wall, unplugged and unattached to other equipment.

I wanted to drop the guitar, grab the recorder, and run for the door, but there were no guarantees that the memory card was in the machine. I picked a few riffs on the guitar and put it back. "That's a nice old guitar. I see you kept Old Red. Still play it?"

Danny's red Gibson Flying V hung on the wall like a trophy. "Not so much these days. I just keep it here for inspiration."

"Like Eddie's old Les Paul, huh? I saw it in the pictures of his studio."

Danny's eyes twitched but he recovered quickly. "Pictures?"

"Yeah," I said. I picked up a Stratocaster and acted more interested in it than the conversation. "That detective—Kearny?—he showed me some pictures the crime techs took when he called me in about the murder. I saw Eddie's Les Paul in the rack with some other guitars. Lots of memories."

"Yeah." Danny's voice got quiet. "Tons of them." A pause, then he bounced back to host mode. "Come on. Let me show the Master Bedroom and then we'll get back downstairs to the gang. We got some celebratin' to do."

I 'm not sure what I expected to see in Danny's bedroom; maybe black light posters and a lava lamp, but I was surprised to find it relatively neat and almost tasteful. I guess of all the rooms in the house, Danny wanted this one to make the best impression. Track lighting bounced off the pale green walls and gave the room a muted glow. The bedroom was dominated by a king-sized four-poster bed and the little brother of the downstairs TV on the opposing wall. The bed was made and covered with a black velour bedspread. Pillows were piled around the headboard and a few spilled onto the floor. On one wall over a tall dresser a frame held a concert poster. Bold red letters spelled out Gin Sing. Just in case the ladies forgot.

Back downstairs, pizza arrived and everybody dug in. I don't eat pizza often, but the sight and scent of a deep crust supreme got the best of me. Besides, I rationalized, I needed to stay sober and a full stomach would offset all the beer I was drinking. I was surprised to see Wendy eating a slice. "Won't that clog your arteries?"

"I'll risk one."

Danny pulled a guitar from behind one of the sofas. He sat on the arm of one of the couches and started strumming along with the CD on the stereo. Two songs later he thumbed the pause button on the remote. "Hey, Sam, how about you playing one?"

Wendy nudged me and said under her breath, "You called that one right." I stood up and reached for the guitar to encouraging shouts and whistles from the guests. It was a pretty nice Washburn. I strummed a few chords, tweaked the tuning a little bit, and spun a couple of quick riffs. Danny said, "How about a sneak peek at the new stuff for the CD?"

I nodded and pulled a chair in front of the television. "Okay, here's one." I kicked up the opening riff of "Watchin' You Walk," a blues rocker that played well as a solo piece but would be dynamite with drums, a Hammond organ and a horn section behind it.

I turned so the Sunsong guys were on the edge of my vision and I was facing Danny head-on. He sat next to Wendy when I moved to the chair and Treecie plopped next to him. When I got to the second verse, I saw one of the Sunsong reps say something in the other's ear. He nodded. They liked the song. I looked over at Wendy and she gave me a brief nod and a smile. When I got to the fourth verse, "When I see you walk into the room, start wrappin' barbed wire 'round my soul," I looked at Danny. He was staring at me as if he'd never seen me before. There was no way could he outgun me on those lyrics.

The song ended to applause. I nodded my appreciation and launched into "Hourglass," a pretty good melody but outstanding lyrics: "Turn me over when you're out of time. I'll fill your emptiness and you fill mine. Run the sand 'til it's gone and then, turn me over let it flow again." Lyrics were Danny's forte, but nothing he could write would top it. The applause was louder this time, and instead of playing a third song, I said, "Let's hear you do one, Danny. How about 'Carry On?'"

Danny hesitated at first, but called up in front of his friends, he had to stand and deliver. He took the guitar from me and we traded places. Wendy put her arm through mine and leaned over. "Good play. He's putting on a game face, but he's not happy about it."

Although Danny was borderline drunk, he managed the intro to "Carry On" with no difficulty. The booze didn't hurt his voice, either. He sang the first verse note perfect and rolled into the chorus without a hitch. Success breeds confidence, and by the end of the second verse, he felt on top again, that is until I chimed in with harmony on the chorus. I stood up and moved over beside him and sang a nice harmony line below his tenor, a line that I'd worked up from the recording of his *Jumpstart* premiere. The Sunsong twins were eating it up. When the song ended, he turned to me. He looked almost shaken. "Where did that come from?"

"I dubbed your act on *Jumpstart* and did my homework." I reached for the guitar. "Can I do one more?"

He nodded and moved back to the sofa. Treecie leaned into him and said something in his ear. He said something over his shoulder, and she sat back like she'd been slapped. I started the opening riff to "One Finger in Ten," the title referring to the finger wearing a wedding ring being outnumbered by the other nine. This time, one of the Sunsong guys was bobbing his torso in time to the music. The other one swayed from side to side. I knew the look on their faces; they were seeing dollar signs. The lyrics were solid, and so was the melody; I punctuated the syncopated chords with string-popping bottom notes that drove the rhythm. The lyrics were a combination of tight rhyme and sharp hooks: "Don't expect that ring to tame me. One finger's only part of one hand. You know I've got another it's my left one's evil brother. I'm nothin' more or less than a man." The applause was even louder this time, and I stood up, bowed to one side then the other.

Danny stood up too, and said to the room at large, "And that's why Sam's coming on board to help me with the new LP." The studio men were nodding in agreement. He turned to me and held out his hand. "Congratulations, Sam. I think you passed the audition." We all laughed at Danny's joke, and he laughed the loudest.

Wendy and I left soon afterward, on Wendy's excuse of an early day at the paper, but not before she got a promise from Danny for an interview. "Call me tomorrow," he said, "and we'll get something going." He kissed her hand like a 19th century viscount. I wanted to punch him and I wanted to laugh at him at the same time. I did neither. I had to remind myself that he was probably a murderer.

35

Wendy was quiet until we were three or four blocks away from Danny's house. "That was really cruel. You let him play his big song and cut in on him. Then you played one more that was even better than your first two, showing him up in front of his friends."

"Not to mention those two hacks from the label. They'll run back to the bosses with the story and I'll write my own contract after tonight. So what did you make of Danny?

"Danny was hard to read; lots of conflict, lots of ambivalence, but he seems to function pretty well under the influence, doesn't he?"

"'Alky's Autopilot,' we call it. I guess he's been drunk and stoned so much for so long that his sense of reality is based on being half in the bag. Watching him try to function while he's sober could be painful. As for the ambivalence, he wants me on board because he needs me and at the same time he hates having me around because I'm better at what I do than he is, and it takes away some of the spotlight. Also, it lets people know that kicking me out of the band years ago was a mistake, and he hates to admit he's wrong."

"I did see him twitch when you mentioned pictures."

"Yeah, I wanted to rattle him a little without tipping my hand. Kearny pulled him in on the investigation too, so I figured that was good cover."

She nodded. "How do you want me to handle the interview?"

"Get him at night if you can, maybe take him to dinner on the paper's dime. Keep him talking to give me the time I need to search the place."

"I think I can manage that."

"I'm sure you can. You managed him pretty well in the party. It doesn't scare you to be with him one-on-one?"

"I've interviewed gang-bangers, mobsters, pimps, coyotes, drug dealers, all kinds of bad guys."

"But no killers?"

"Tony Scaglione supposedly cut up three live ones with a chainsaw; never proven of course. I interviewed him about union violence once. He was a perfect gentleman with me. Does he count?"

I nodded. "I guess so. You earned your stripes. I suppose after that parade of crooks you won't have trouble with Danny."

"He'll be easy; I'll just lead him around by the ego. He's a lecherous creep, but I've managed worse. He doesn't think he has as much to fear from me as he does from you, Sam. At least that's how he sees things; it's the chauvinism. Speaking of easy, you seem to be taking this all very casually. You're about to commit burglary and you treat it like an everyday event. Have you done this before?"

"That would be telling, wouldn't it?" I smiled at her. "Allow me a little mystery. And no, I'm not casual about it at all. We're playing for keeps here, and we have to do it right. If I seem calm, it's because I can't afford to be afraid. This game is like riding a motorcycle; if you let it scare you and something goes wrong, you panic and it gets you killed. I'm counting on you to help me make it work. And just in case..."

I opened the console and pulled out a small velvet bag tied with a braided gold cord. I handed it to her and I could tell she knew what it was before she opened the bag. She pulled out a two-shot Derringer. "It's a .32, a little insurance to carry in your purse. You ever shoot one before?"

"A pistol? Hell yes. I carried one in Tucson for a while when I had some death threats. That one was a revolver." She shook the bag and the bullets rattled inside.

"There's no safety. Cock the hammer, fire it and cock it again. The firing pin shifts to the second barrel. I figured that was the easiest to hide in your bag. Not very accurate, but close-up, it'll do the job."

"How do you know I don't have one now?"

"It's not safe to make assumptions; I looked in your purse. I want to be sure you have an edge."

When we got back to my place, I invited Wendy in to finish the chardonnay but she passed on it, saying her early morning excuse was for real. "Thanks, Sam for an interesting evening." She leaned across the console and kissed me, and I felt a sad sense of déjà vu as she drove away. Maybe I scared her the other night; maybe she scared herself. She'll still be there when this is over, I told myself. In the meantime, I've got a killer to catch.

36

I didn't sleep well that night. I kept waking up breathing hard from dreams I couldn't remember. I finally gave up around five o'clock and dragged myself into the kitchen. I stuck two slices of bread in the toaster and put on coffee. I slathered the toast with peanut butter and took the works into the living room where I sat on the couch and stared at the blank television screen. If this were a movie, what would the hero do? How would Mike Hammer, Philip Marlowe, or Sam Spade move on the case? They'd do what I was doing, tiptoe around the cops and look for clues. But they would also bust heads, rattle teeth, and shake loose what they needed to know. Wendy said it: this was reality. I had no private eye license, no authority at all to do what I was doing, and while I was no wimp, I was no major league tough guy either. I could probably go to jail for withholding evidence or obstructing an investigation, and for what? An abstraction: Justice.

I was convinced that Danny killed Eddie and Lottie. I had to prove it with hard evidence; the why would come later. Did I really care that much about Eddie? Or Lottie for that matter? Maybe, maybe not, but something inside me twisted my guts when I thought about Danny walking away from it all smiling his crooked grin. I wanted to put my fist through that grin, but that would last for only a minute. Murder was forever, and justice demanded that retribution last forever too.

● ● ●

Cotton called a few hours later. "You got your meeting."

"At the jail?"

"They said to bring you to the Sperry Avenue Social Club at noon. I guess Blue Smoke's attorney talked the judge into bail. You oughta feel privileged, Sam. They don't usually let white folks through the door."

The Sperry Avenue Social Club was the flip side of Bendik's in Raisford, Hanniston's ghetto, and the home base for Lavalle Grooms' uncle, Tiny Settles. Tiny ran the black side of the drug trade in Hanniston. Everyone knew it, and Tiny stayed in business by paying off anyone with an open hand and cutting off the hands that closed in a fist; the age-old pair: carrots and Styx. Like it or not, Sperry was where I would find my answers.

"Do I meet you there?"

"No, they want to make sure you arrive. They told me to bring you in my car. I'll pick you up in an hour. I got to say, Sam, you got more balls than most people."

I hung up and got a beer from the fridge. Balls? I wanted to jump out of my skin and run away from it all at that moment, but I knew I couldn't let myself do that. And if I didn't show, they'd come looking for me because now I was on their radar. I poured the beer down the kitchen sink and picked up my guitar and played it for the longest hour of my life.

Cotton was late, which didn't help my frame of mind. He pulled up in his blue Lincoln Town Car and opened the passenger door. "Sorry, man; traffic."

I slid into the seat beside him. "I see you dressed for the occasion." He was wearing a pale green suit, probably from the night before, over a pale blue shirt. I wore my usual jeans and denim shirt under a leather jacket. Any other day I'd've bantered with him about his classy ride and how much more playing the sax pays than playing the guitar, but not today. "Get me there on time, Cotton. Don't keep our friends waiting."

He wheeled out into the street and headed north through Pembroke and Shady Hills. Looking out the window, I could see the progressive disintegration of the city as we moved from the working class neighborhoods through the slums and into a world I'd never seen. Raisford was a shock; it made me think of post-apocalyptic movies; shells of buildings, empty lots from burn downs overgrown with weeds and cluttered with hulks of cars and rubble. I expected to see zombies staggering around the next corner, but what I saw instead were people, all too alive, feral; conditioned by a lifetime of surviving in an urban jungle and living by its unique rules. Their eyes followed the Lincoln as we wheeled past, and I was convinced that if Cotton dropped me off on a street corner here, I probably wouldn't walk out of Raisford alive.

The Sperry Avenue Social Club was a concrete block building, no windows, one big, flat story surrounded by a cracked asphalt parking lot that took up half of a city block. There were no cars out front, and Cotton pulled up to the door, where two black men waited.

"Here you are. Good luck, Sam."

"Aren't you coming in?"

"They said they wanted to see you. They got no reason to see me."

I took a deep breath and let it out. I stepped out of the car, and strode as casually as I could to the waiting pair of bouncers. One was tall and lean, dressed in a shabby blue suit with yellow suspenders. I could see the butt of a pistol sticking out of the waist band of his trousers, no attempt to conceal it. He smiled and a golden front tooth with the embossed letters JR flashed in the sunlight. The other man was one big muscle, his short-cropped hair merging with a full beard. I didn't see a gun on him. He probably didn't need one.

JR patted me down. I stood as perfectly still as if a scorpion were crawling up my arm. He opened my wallet and thumbed through my cash and cards then handed it back to me. He said to the beard, "He's clean."

The heavy steel door opened and I stepped from the daylight into the heart of darkness. The bar area just inside the door was unlit except for a few beer signs on the walls and the flash of a jukebox thumping out hip-hop. I could see booths lining the walls and tables and the silhouettes of two more men sitting with their backs to the bar. JR put a hand on my shoulder and lightly turned me to the left. "This way."

He rapped on another steel door. It swung inward, and I found myself in a room empty except for a plain table and three chairs. A shaded light fixture hung over the table, leaving the edges of the room in shadow. It reminded me of Kearny's interrogation room, but less friendly. JR steered me to one of the chairs and said, "Have a seat." I did, and I sat back in the chair and put my palms flat on the table. No sudden moves. When the door shut I could barely hear the hip-hop from the bar. In less than a minute, a door opened on the other side of the room. I expected Lavalle

Grooms. What I got was Tiny Settles, all three hundred pounds of him.

Tiny strode into the room with an unexpected grace for his size. He was about six feet tall and four feet wide, heavy with that hard fat over muscle you see on old pro football players and body builders gone to seed. His belly strained the buttons of his red silk shirt. Tiny sat in the chair on the other side of the table and stared at me like an angry Buddha without speaking, maybe waiting for me to break the silence. I knew better. His hair was shot with grey and I marveled that he'd lived so long in his profession.

He reached under the table and pulled out a bottle of Wild Turkey and two shot glasses. He poured two drinks and set one between my hands. I didn't move. "Drink?"

I shook my head and smiled. "Not now, thanks."

"When you're ready." He tipped his back and downed it in one pull. Then he slammed the shot glass onto the table with a crack as loud as a gunshot. I didn't flinch. He tipped his basketball of a head back and looked at me from the bottom of his eyes. "Now, white boy." His voice was a low gravelly rumble. "What you want with my nephew?"

I met his stare with one of my own. "The cops think Blue Smoke killed Eddie Shay. I think different, and maybe I can prove it. Blue Smoke knows things I don't. I figure maybe we can help each other."

"What do you care about some nigger drug dealer, white boy?"

"I don't care about him much at all. What I care about is the man who pulled the trigger."

"And why's that?"

"Because he killed a friend of mine to cover it up."

Tiny thought that one over and nodded his head. "We'll see about that." He twitched his head to the bearded man who went out the door behind me to a blast from the jukebox and Tiny and I sat watching each other. Neither of us spoke. I felt a bead of sweat trickle along the ridge of my spine. Keep it simple, I told myself. Just tell the truth. Unfortunately for me, the truth was anything but simple.

A moment later the music got loud again and with it, I heard scuffling feet. The beard and one of the men from the bar had Cotton by the arms, dragging him into the room. He blurted out, "Mr. Settles, I…" Tiny cut him off with a simple gesture; without looking at Cotton, he raised his index finger. I didn't want to speculate about what happened if he got past two fingers to three. JR dragged the empty chair around to Tiny's side of the table and the other two slammed Cotton into it. Cotton's eyes were wild, like the eyes of a rabbit in the jaws of a panther. Neither of us counted on this twist.

"You're a pretty cool customer, Dunne," Tiny said, "when it's your own white ass in the chair. Let's see how much you care about *this* friend." One of the men holding Cotton grabbed him by the ears and the other took and a handful of his hair and his chin, locking his head.

Tiny reached into his pocket and pulled out a straight razor. It was an antique, ivory handled with silver filigree. "This was my granddaddy's razor." He looked at it and spoke with fondness in his voice. "It's a beautiful thing. He taught me how to use it when I was a little boy." Tiny's eyes locked into mine. "Then he taught me how to use it all over again when I become a man." He thumbed the handle, and the blade swung out like the Reaper's scythe.

He reached across the table and lightly drew the razor across the back of my index finger. He held my eyes the whole time, and I didn't break the stare. I barely felt a pinch, but in a second, blood began to weal from a hairline cut.

"That's just to let you know this ain't for show." He turned to Cotton and with one hand pulled out his lower lip between his thumb and forefinger. With the other, he held the razor at the corner of Cotton's mouth. He looked at me and not at Cotton. "Now, white boy, you talk to me and talk to me straight, or your friend here won't be playin' the saxophone no more. What you want with my nephew?"

I've been blessed all my life that panic doesn't exist in my emotional repertoire, but this scene was pushing my limits. I took a long breath. "I need to know who Blue Smoke sold dope to the night of Eddie Shay's murder. I say he sold to the killer. I say Blue Smoke didn't kill anybody. I say he did his business and went on his way. I say maybe he was set up. I need to know who and when so I can hang the sonofabitch who did it."

"And who is this killer?"

"I don't know yet, but I'm getting close."

Tiny never moved. Tears were welling up in Cotton's eyes.

"So he tells you what you want to know. What then?"

"It aims me at the proof I need. When I have it, Blue Smoke walks on the murder charge. The killer goes down instead. Blue Smoke's going inside for the coke anyway, so what does it matter if he fingers one customer? Besides, he can trade it with the cops for shorter time."

Tiny's eyes slid to the side for a second and back to me. "And how do I know I can trust you to do this?"

We'd reached a tipping point; he liked the idea and he was looking for reassurance. I spun the wheel. "Because this is your town and I live in it.

And three or four nights a week I'm sitting in a spotlight playing my guitar. You couldn't find an easier target. And if you don't kill me in a bar or club, you'll shoot me in the parking lot, or walking down the street with a drive-by, or in Burger King. That's how you know."

For a long moment Tiny stared me down, then he let go of Cotton's lip and closed the razor. Tiny nodded and his men let go of Cotton's head. Cotton sagged in the chair as if someone had pulled a plug and let the air out of him.

"JR, take him out and send Lavalle in here."

My hands were still flat on the table. "I'll have that drink now, if you don't mind."

Tiny didn't exactly smile; his eyes crinkled a little at the corners. "I knew you would."

In a minute the door opened and Blue Smoke came in. He wasn't wearing his pusher's uniform; he was wearing jeans, a Chicago Bulls jersey and two hundred dollar basketball shoes. He wasn't Blue Smoke the Diamond Dealer anymore; he was an overgrown kid in trouble over his head and scared as hell. He looked smaller than he did on TV, but maybe that was just a comparison with Tiny. "Sit down, Lavalle."

Grooms looked at me with the kind of curiosity you'd expect to see for a man from Mars. "Who's he?"

"This man is going to help you beat the murder rap. Tell him what he needs to know."

Lavalle looked at me and back to his uncle. Tiny gave a slow, confirming nod.

Lavalle turned back to me. "What you need?"

I said, "We both know you're going inside for dealing, so you don't have to deny that. The night of the murder, three weeks ago Tuesday, who did you sell to?"

He shook his head. "You put that out of your mind soon as you drive away, man. I couldn't tell you who I sold to three nights ago."

"Ever go to their houses?"

"No way. I work strictly out the window."

"Okay, how about names of your customers? If I name names, could you tell me whether you sold to them?"

"Shit. They don't have names. I give 'em nicknames. They call my cell, give me the nickname, tell me what they want, I say where and when. I don't want to know their real names."

I nodded. "Door number three: if I show you some pictures, could you tell me if maybe they were customers?"

Before he could answer, I nodded toward my hands. "Pictures in my shirt pocket." Tiny nodded. I pulled out a packet of photos held by a rubber band. The first was a picture of a local politician clipped from the *Sentinel*. I put it face up on the table. "Him?"

Grooms leaned in close. He was taking it seriously. He studied it for a few seconds and said, "Not him."

Next was a snapshot of an old girlfriend.

"No. Don't sell to many bitches. Too much hassle."

The third was a newspaper picture of a city councilman. "Call him 'Dumbo' 'cause of his ears. Yeah, I sold to him, but not for a while."

I showed him five more and got two positives; a local jeweler and a lawyer whose web address was suethebastards.com, "Hazy" and "Shaft," respectively.

The next picture was Danny Barton.

"Miami."

"Miami?"

"That's what I nickname him, 'cause he had a stubble beard like that dude on the TV show."

"You sold to him?"

"Sometimes. If that's him. Look like him. I can't say for sure about the night of the murder, but he's a regular."

I nodded. "One more." I laid down a picture of Eddie.

"That the dead guy?"

"That's him."

"The cops showed me pictures of him too. I never seen the man in my life, let alone sell to him."

Tiny had been watching Grooms closely the whole time. "Anything else you can tell the man?"

Lavalle shook his and lowered his eyes under Tiny's stare. "No, sir."

Tiny pointed to the door and Lavalle left without another word.

Tiny turned to me. "You think one of them killed your friend?"

"It's all maybes right now, but I'm not letting it go. The cops might, but I won't."

"When will you know?"

"Soon."

"You'll tell Cotton?"

"As soon as I know, you'll know. That's the best I can give you."

Tiny pointed to the pictures. "If it was me, maybe I'd just kill all of 'em, but that wouldn't help Lavalle much." Tiny pulled out a thick roll of bills

"You sold to him?"

with a hundred on the outside and pushed it across the table to me. "Take that in case you need it. You don't, keep it." I stood up and pocketed the money. I could have turned it down, but I didn't want to risk insulting Tiny. "He's my sister's only child. Cut him loose, Dunne."

Tiny didn't have to tell me what could happen if I didn't. Like "The Ballad of Louie Alexander" puts it: *A gift from the Devil is a debt in the end.*

JR escorted me back through the bar and into the sunlight. Cotton was slumped behind the wheel of the Lincoln. When I got in, I saw that he'd thrown up on his suit.

"Goddammit, Sam! I thought you were gonna get us killed."

"Sometimes you have to roll the dice, Cotton."

"Yeah, well I ain't gonna be one of them dice next time. I'll be spendin' all night with my sponsor as it is."

We cruised through the combat zone without speaking. Cotton slowed for a red light, and two young toughs ran up to our windows pointing guns. "Out of the car! Now!"

"Oh shit." Cotton was reaching for the door handle when I heard a horn honk. A black Suburban roared up behind us. The doors opened and the guards from the Social Club stepped out with sawed off shotguns. The carjackers looked at them and ran. The light turned green and Cotton floored it. Safe passage: a professional courtesy from Tiny.

37

Wendy called around five o'clock.

"I had quite a day." I told her. "I had a sit down with Lavalle Grooms." I paused, "and Tiny Settles."

Wendy didn't say anything for a minute. "Since you're still able to talk, I assume it went well?"

I told her about the Sperry incident. She didn't say a word. I wondered if she were writing it all down. When I finished the story, I said, "How about you? Ready for tonight?"

Wendy said she would meet Danny at Valozzi's, a local restaurant at eight for the interview. I checked an online almanac. The sun would set around 6:45. By eight it would be just about dark and I'd have a good shot at Danny's house without being seen. She would text me when he arrived and call me once the interview was over.

"I don't see any risk to me. It's a public place, and he has no reason to suspect me of anything. I'll insist on eating dinner before the interview and maybe have a drink after to stretch things as long as I can. You should have a good ninety minutes from the time he arrives 'til we're done. If you're out sooner, text me."

Ninety minutes should do it. It was unlikely he'd moved the recorder, and if the data card was in it, I could have my proof. The data card would have Danny's prints on it for sure; I was hoping it would have Eddie's prints on it too. If Danny didn't erase the song, I could take the works to Kearny and he could make a case. Also, if I didn't have to hunt for the recorder or the card, I'd have time to look for a .38.

I dressed in black for my expedition to Danny's house; black trousers, black T-shirt under a black jacket, and even black Reeboks. On Razor's advice I bought a black ski mask. "You're more recognizable than you think, man. Besides, you've been to the house before. Somebody might show up who saw you that night and finger you." I pulled it over my head and adjusted the eyeholes. It itched. Looking at myself in the mirror, I felt like an idiot for about ten seconds and then I felt like a secret agent.

I put the lock picks in a pocket of the jacket and zipped it shut. A small flashlight went into another. I covered most the face of the flashlight with electrical tape to narrow its beam. Sandwich sized baggies and latex gloves went into a third pocket. I clipped the Beretta in my waistband at the small of my back, just in case, and pulled my shirt over it. Time to roll.

I got to Danny's neighborhood around 7:45 and parked a block away in front of a house with a realtor's sign in the front yard and no lights in the windows. Eight o'clock came and went; no text from Wendy. Danny was late, I figured, and I settled down to wait. At a quarter past eight, the text came: "Here."

It was dark by now and I was able to slip unnoticed through the alley to Danny's garage. No lights were on in the house. I tiptoed through the backyard and looked around the corner to the driveway. No cars.

The back porch was dark enough that I wouldn't be seen, and dark enough that I had to hold the flashlight in my teeth while I worked the lock. I put on my gloves and went to work. The lock was stubborn, and I was sweating by the time I got it open. I stepped inside and closed the door behind me. The alarm system keypad glowed green in the mud room: System activated. Green digits were counting down from 60. I punched in the code from memory; the readout blinked twice: System deactivated.

I picked my way carefully through the kitchen and took the back stairs to the second floor, walking on the outsides of the stair treads to minimize noise. The house was silent, but I was taking no chances.

The jam room door was closed. I tried the knob and found it unlocked. The jam room looked pretty much as I saw it before, guitars on the wall and in floor stands, amplifiers and p.a. speakers scattered around the floor and plenty of cable to trip over. I picked my way carefully around it all, relying on the beam from the penlight. I missed one cable, and I tripped on it, pitching forward and knocking over an empty guitar stand. It clattered on the floor and I cursed under my breath. I stood still listening for a full minute before I moved again.

The recorder was where I saw it before, on a table unplugged and propped against the wall. I tiptoed to the table and opened the sliding door to the card slot. In the beam of the flashlight, I could see the edge of the card. I reached in with my thumb and forefinger to pull it out.

The lights came on.

"Sonofabitch!" A naked man, his torso covered in tattoos, charged through the doorway swinging a baseball bat. I recognized his face and stringy hair from the night before. His sweat and wild eyes said PCP.

I ducked in time to avoid his first swing, the bat whistling over my head, but his backswing glanced off my forehead. I saw stars and reeled against the wall. I would have pulled the Beretta to warn him off, but I never had the chance.

He snarled and raised the bat over his head to club me, and I swiveled into him and crushed his bare toes with my boot heel. He screamed but didn't drop the bat. I caught him on the chin with an uppercut. His teeth clipped together, his head jerked back, and he and the bat hit the floor. He tried to raise his head, but his eyes rolled back and he was out.

Silence. Nobody else in the house, thank God. I pulled the data card from the recorder and put it in one of the baggies. I shut off the room light and left the Illustrated Man on the floor. I dashed down the back steps. I couldn't stick around to look for the gun.

I didn't bother resetting the alarm code or the relocking the deadbolt. I ran to the van, started it up and drove for five minutes before I stopped at red light and saw people staring from the car beside me. I realized I was still wearing the ski mask. When the light turned, they pulled away a little faster than necessary, and I pulled off the mask. My forehead was throbbing over my right eye and I could feel a lump starting.

By nine o'clock I was sitting in a McDonalds' parking lot holding a chocolate milkshake against my forehead. I was praying Danny's buddy didn't wake up before he got home. I checked my pockets. Nothing missing.

I took everything out of the house I took into it. And I got the data card. I texted Wendy: "Out." I kicked the seat back and waited for almost an hour for her call.

"We're done. He's pulling out now."

"How did it go?"

"The interview was easy. Beyond a few anecdotes there really isn't much to him, but I feel like I need two showers. He really came onto me."

"No surprise there."

"Did you get the card?"

"Yeah, but when Danny gets home, all hell's gonna break loose." I filled her in about Danny's house guest and my truncated mission.

"You were lucky he didn't have a gun. So now what?"

"So now you meet me at Eddie's house. I have to find out what's on that card, and then we go talk to Kearny. I can't stall anymore. When the tattooed guy wakes up, he'll tell Danny about the break in, and even Danny can figure out what's up. On the plus side, he won't call the cops."

"Why not?"

"If he realizes what's missing, he'll be desperate to get it back. Besides, he can't risk the cops processing his party house as a crime scene. Too many drugs." I gave her Eddie's address and she said she'd be there in a few minutes, no questions asked. She wanted to be in on the payoff. I could have gone to Eddie's by myself to use the Rec-Tech, but after my adventure at Danny's I was gun-shy. I wanted someone to watch my back when I went in.

38

Wendy pulled into Eddie's driveway twenty minutes later and cut the lights. I waited until a passing car turned the corner at the end of the block and stepped out of the shadows. I tapped on the Acura's passenger window. She unlocked the door and I slid in beside her. "Where's your car?"

"I parked it a block away. Too many cars in the driveway might attract attention." I pulled the stolen keys out of my pocket.

"Do you want me to move?"

"No, wait here. This won't take long. If the cops drive by, or one of the neighbors comes out, tap the horn." She nodded and I slipped out the passenger door. I was in the house in less than a minute and heading for Eddie's studio. I left the door unlocked in case I had to make a quick getaway.

I tiptoed through the passageway between the kitchen and the studio in the dark and pulled the door shut behind me. I figured lights in the studio would be safe because of the heavy drapes, so I switched on the rack of fluorescents at the back of the room. I pulled the memory card from my pocket and slipped it into the slot in the recorder, holding it by the edges so I wouldn't smudge any prints. This time when I powered up the recorder, the readout showed a song. It took me a minute to trace the wires to the right amplifier and switch it on. Then I pressed Play on the Rec-Tech.

I heard a count-in and the soft rock arpeggios of Eddie's guitar. It was "You and Me." The bass and drums kicked in, and a little bit of string. Then Eddie's voice skated over the backup tracks like Nancy Kerrigan. "You and me, we walked a long mile together…" Lottie was right, Eddie's song and Eddie's arrangement were winners. I pictured him, a smile on his face, the ring on his middle finger and a cigarette between three and four, making music, not money.

The studio door latch clicked. "It's a great song, isn't it?" Startled, I spun to see Danny in the doorway with an arm around Wendy's neck and a gun to her head. It was a short barreled .38 and I was ready to bet it was the same one that killed Eddie and Lottie. I didn't hear them come in the house between the music and the soundproofing.

He pushed her ahead of him into the room. Wendy looked more angry than frightened. "I didn't hear him, Sam. He…"

Danny tightened his arm, cutting off her sentence. "Shut, up."

I stepped away from the recording equipment and looked him in the eye. "Yeah, it's a great song. Too bad you didn't write it, but I'm not surprised. You never had half the talent Eddie did. Why the hell did you do this?"

"You know what it's like, Sam, if anybody would. No, maybe not, because you never made it. Once you have, you can't ever let it go. Eddie wanted it all for himself; he was going to leave me like he left you…"

"You mean like both of you left me."

Danny ignored me and kept going. He was on a crazy, coke-fueled roll. Wendy squirmed and tried to slam his chin with the back of her head, but all she did was knock his glasses loose. They hung to the side from one ear. His eyes shone with a cold gleam like moonlight on the edge of a knife. I could see through them to the merry-go-rounds turning inside his skull.

"He called me up and said to come over. He said he had some news. Yeah, he had news all right; he said once the last CD was in the can, he was making a break. He was breaking my balls is what he was breaking. And I tried to reason with him, but he wouldn't hear me. He put on that song…" Music still poured from the monitors. He pointed to the speaker array with his pistol.

"'You and Me.'"

"No, man, not 'You and Me,' 'Carry On!' Shut it off, Sam." Louder, "Shut it off!"

I raised my hands slowly, palms forward, to chest height, reached back and pushed the Stop button on the recorder. The sudden silence was jarring.

"He said this was his ticket to a solo career. He said, 'You and I had a good run, Danny, but it's over,' like I was one of his bimbo girlfriends or something. He was throwing me away after fifteen years like a used Kleenex!"

If I was lucky, I could grab for the Beretta in my waistband and maybe get a shot off. My big worry was hitting Wendy. The little automatic wasn't exactly a target gun. Keep him talking. "And for that you killed him?"

His breath was almost a pant. "You don't know what it means, Sam. You never made it to the top. It's like being a god. And Eddie was going to just yank it out from under me. I begged him. I told him I'd give him my share of the royalties, anything, but he wouldn't listen. I pulled the gun, and you know what he did? He laughed at me. Laughed at me! He was killing me and he thought it was all a joke!"

"So you killed him instead, and you're still shit out of luck."

"I didn't think. I just snapped and pulled the trigger. Next thing I knew, he was on the floor. The walls sucked up the sound. The neighbors never heard it. And they won't hear it tonight, either."

I let that one slide. "And the coke?"

"The drug thing was a happy accident," he rambled. "I was so freaked out after I shot Eddie that I just sat here on the floor for a while. Anybody walked in would've found me. My stash was in a little metal tin, and when I pulled it out of my pocket, it fell and rolled away and spilled all over the floor. It's funny how things fall into place. When I saw the coke on the floor, I got the idea to take his money out of his wallet."

Somewhere in the middle of this torrent of words Wendy stopped struggling. She was taking in every detail. This would be the story of a lifetime—if she lived to write it. I could see calculation in her eyes that Danny couldn't.

"And Eddie's ring?"

"I took it. I figured it would look like a bum drug deal. And then to nail it down, I called that rolling pusher."

"Blue Smoke."

"Yeah, Blue Smoke. He took my money and when he reached for the coke, he couldn't see me flip the ring behind his seat. And it worked, just like a movie."

Keep him talking. "Okay, I get Eddie, but why did you kill Lottie?"

"She called me right after I was on *Jumpstart*. She said, 'We need to talk—you and me,' and she hung up. She said that, and I knew she knew, maybe not about the murder but about the song. I went to her place and she told me Eddie played that goddamned song for her when she took his pictures. Eddie never did that before. He never let anybody hear our songs. I tried to tell her I worked with him on it, but she wasn't buying it." He was talking faster now, the words tumbling out.

"I said, 'What do you want from me?' and she never said what she wanted. She didn't say, 'I want money.' She didn't say, 'I want a new Pentax.' She didn't say, 'I want you to marry me.' You know what she said? She said, 'I'll think it over,' and that scared me more than anything. I knew right then she was gonna be a bottomless pit for the rest of my life—or hers. I turned up the stereo to cover the gunshot, and when I turned to shoot her, do you know what she did? She took my picture holding the fucking gun."

"That's why you cleaned out her camera."

"Yeah." Danny laughed a high-pitched giggle. "You shoulda seen me stumblin' down the fire stairs. Anybody coulda seen me any second. It was all just dumb luck that I got away with it."

Time to roll the dice. "So now what? You gonna kill me too? And her? And the cops, and the fans, and the whole wide world? Let her go, Danny."

"Little miss newsprint?" He sneered. "No way. Playin' me for a sucker with that phony interview. I fell for it too, but I followed her afterward to see where she lived, and what does she do? She drives to Eddie's house. And there you were. You should've just taken my offer, Sam. Now I can't let either of you walk out of here."

"Come on, Danny; this has nothing to do with her. This is just between you and me. It always was." My eyes flicked at Wendy. I could see her hand slipping under her blouse. Too bad Danny caught it too, because when she pulled the derringer, he slashed his pistol down across the back of her hand and her gun clattered on the floor. The distraction gave me the chance I needed to grab for the Beretta. I leveled it at Danny's skull. He pulled Wendy around as a shield.

"Put it down, Sam, or I'll put one in her head."

"Yeah? And then I'll put one in your friggin' eyeball. I can't miss from here." It was pure bravado. I'd be lucky if I hit him at all. He cocked his hammer and I cocked mine. Wendy's eyes bulged.

"Don't make me laugh. You won't shoot me."

"But I will." Kearny stood half shadowed in the studio doorway aiming his Glock.

Danny panicked and swung left toward Kearny, putting Wendy between them and snapped off two shots before Kearny could fire. Kearny had no cover in that narrow hallway between the kitchen and the studio, and he went down. Wendy jabbed an elbow into Danny's gut and twisted away, giving me a clear shot. I fired three times, and Danny dropped his gun and clawed at his throat. He fell over backward and I crossed the room.

My wild shots hit Danny in his left side with one bullet and nicked an artery in his neck with another. Blood spurted between his fingers. His free hand spider crawled across the floor to his right. Even dying, the crazy bastard was groping for Wendy's derringer. I put my foot on his hand and pressed it to the floor. I kicked the derringer out of Danny's reach and stood over him, gulping air. I pointed my gun at his face.

"Like I said about your eye…"

"No!" Wendy shouted. "You shoot him again, it's murder!"

I thought it over; she had a point: murder with a cop and a reporter as eyewitnesses. I thumbed down the hammer on my pistol. Then I hauled off and kicked Danny in the face like I'd kick a field goal. It felt almost as good. "That was for Lottie."

I turned to the doorway where Kearny sprawled with Wendy kneeling beside him. He was hit in the shoulder, and she was stanching the blood with that stupid striped necktie.

Kearny croaked, "Call 911 and tell them 'officer down.'"

In a few minutes, the place was swarming with cops. Nothing brings them running like a bullet in one of their own. They ran the crime scene and took my statement and my gun while the paramedics hauled Kearny away on a gurney and the medical examiner hauled Danny away in a bag. Somehow Wendy disappeared in the shuffle, professional courtesy, I suppose. She had a story to write.

39

The sun was coming up when I walked out the front door of the precinct station. No charges were filed against me; Kearny saw to that, but I'll probably never see my Beretta or the derringer again. Maybe I'll buy a Glock this time. Kearny heard enough of Danny's rant to know who did what, and I was sure the slug from Kearny's shoulder would match the ones from Eddie and Lottie. Case closed.

Wendy was waiting for me in the parking lot.

"You file your story?"

She nodded. "The paper's doing a special edition. They're replating the front page and putting it on the street this afternoon."

"I can't wait for your interview on *Jumpstart*."

"As soon as Donna Fields finishes mourning."

"In the meantime, there's always *60 Minutes*."

She shook her head. "More like *Entertainment Tonight*."

"Hungry?"

"Hungry enough."

"Dora's?"

"Why not?"

We walked into Dora's and Jenny was behind the counter as usual. Wendy walked past her ahead of me, and Jenny reached over the counter and grabbed my sleeve. She touched the bruise on my forehead with a finger. "Rough night, huh?"

I said, "You have no idea."

She tilted her head and looked at me from the tops of her eyes. "I warned you."

In the booth, Wendy and I didn't say much. Life swirled on around us as if we hadn't just made major news; we were enjoying that last quiet moment before the world discovered us.

People respond to death in different ways. When the food arrived, I tore into my plate of bacon and hash browns as if somebody were going to take it away from me while Wendy picked at her omelet. I could see that Wendy had something on her mind, so I waited for her to bring it up. The wait was a short one.

"You scared me last night, Sam."

"Why, because you saw me kill somebody?"

She shook her head. "Believe it or not, that was no surprise. I might have killed Danny myself if he hadn't knocked the gun out of my hand. It's what you said to him. You said, 'This is just between us; it always has been.' And there I was with his arm around my neck and a gun to my head. I wasn't even part of the equation."

I set my fork down and looked her in the eye. "If I dropped the gun or if I never pulled on him at all, he would have killed us both."

"But Kearny came."

"Yeah, and he got shot for his trouble. And how would I know he'd show up?"

"You couldn't have known, but I did because I called him."

"You called Kearny?" I leaned forward. "When?"

"As soon as you went into Eddie's house I called Mike on my cell phone. I figured you had the proof you needed and it was time to tell him what you suspected and what you knew. Trouble is I had my window partway down so I could listen for cars, and Danny was a quiet sonofabitch. I never heard him sneak up on me, but I guess he heard enough of my conversation. The next thing I knew, he had a gun in my ear and he was yanking me out of the car. But I did honk the horn."

"And I didn't hear it. I forgot about the soundproofing." I took a drink of my coffee. "So you play your angle. You call Kearny and you're off the hook for holding out on him. If there's a bag left to hold, I own it. What if Kearny came to the party five minutes late? Every second I kept the ball in the air was one more second we stayed alive. I made a judgment call and we got lucky."

She thought that one over. "You got what you wanted, though, didn't you? You talked a lot about putting Danny behind bars or on the table, but what you really wanted was to kill him yourself. Mike was on the floor bleeding, and all you cared about was putting another bullet in Danny. And it wasn't just Danny or Eddie or Lottie. You were getting even for your whole screwed-up life."

I had no answer for that one.

"I was a pawn, Sam. So was Mike. So was Cotton. That's the trouble with you. You dance with a couple of toes over the edge all the time, even when somebody's holding your hand to get pulled over with you. You're dangerous." She stood up. "I'll have to think about you for a while."

"Likewise."

She blinked. "What?"

Three count. "I'll have to think about me for a while too." Wendy walked out and left me alone in the booth. I had a call to make. "Cotton?"

"Yeah, Sam?" He was wide awake; probably hadn't gone to bed yet.

"Tell our friend Mr. Settles that Lavalle is clear on the murder charge. I'll fill you in later."

I shut the phone and stared for a while into my coffee pondering the truth of what Wendy said. Then Jenny plopped down on the empty bench. She gave me her Lauren Hutton smile and said, "Is this seat taken?"

I laid my hand on the table palm up and she laid hers palm down on top of it. My fingers closed on hers. "Let me tell you a story . . ."

40

Wendy didn't call that night, or the day after. The special edition of the *Sentinel* carried the headline "Sentinel Reporter in Murder Shootout" over the fold on page one. The *Herald* grudgingly carried the story on the front page the next day under the headline "Shay Murderer Killed." This time they spelled my name right. The TV and radio newsies were reading Wendy's first-person account verbatim over the air. I let her have the spotlight. I was happy enough that it was over. Joe fielded the press calls for me, and a few days later I released a simple statement:

I regret having to kill Danny Barton to defend myself and others. That act will haunt me for the rest of my life. Some may say that justice is served, but our world is never served by the death of any creative person, no matter what his crimes. We are always poorer for the loss.

Cotton agreed with me later that I topped Danny's eulogy on the horseshit meter.

Kearny's shoulder was pretty busted up. He needed surgery to screw his bones back together and that bought him a week at Carson Memorial Hospital. I went to see him a few days after his operation. He was propped up in bed. A cast covered him from hips to throat and ran down his right arm. Kearny was reading a Stephen King paperback and had one of those kidney-shaped spit trays on his chest. His Skoal can was on the nightstand.

"I thought you'd be reading *Police Gazette*. Improving your mind?"

"What's to improve?" He set the book aside and motored his bed up a few degrees. "So when were you going to tell me about Lottie's pictures, the extra copyright form and the data card?"

"When I was sure I had enough proof that Barton wasn't going to wiggle out of it somehow—circumstantial evidence and all that."

"Don't try this at home, kids. There's a reason they call that show *Jackass.* You damn near got us all killed. When I get out of this bed, I'm gonna kick *your* ass. That and bust you for two B and Es." His head lolled back on the pillow, eyes aimed at the ceiling.

"No rush."

"So how's Wendy?" The question surprised me. I guess she wasn't talking much to Kearny right now either.

"In her glory, I guess. I haven't heard from her for a while. She's getting her fifteen minutes and then some. Word is she has an agent working on a book deal already."

"She's tough. She'll handle it all and never break a sweat. It took a while, but I figured out she was playing me and helping you to land herself a big story."

"And I thought she was playing me and helping you."

Kearny pushed his lip and nodded. "She's good."

"Triangulation. I have her version; she called you without telling me and you showed up. How did you get there so fast?"

"Pure luck. I was on my way home and maybe ten minutes away from Shay's house when she called me."

"You live in Banner Heights on your salary?"

He lowered one eyebrow. "No, but believe it or not, I do have a few friends who make more money than I do. Anyway, I get to Shay's and she's not in the car. I didn't call it in because she said it was just the two of you. I go to the front door and find it open, I go in, and you know the rest."

"Not quite." I said, leaning in. "How long were you listening in the doorway?"

"Not long, but long enough to get the drift of the conversation."

"So you could have taken him down any time, but you waited." I considered adding, and let Danny rant while he had a gun to Wendy's head, but I didn't.

Kearny closed his eyes as if running the scene in his head. "He held her between you two and I had a clean shot at him, at least until you forced the play. When you pulled on him, procedure went off the table. I had to wing it."

"And you got winged in the bargain." I rapped on his cast with my knuckles. "Well, we all got what we wanted, right? You solved a double, Wendy got her story, and I got justice. What's not to like?"

Kearny spat in the tray. "You know, if he hadn't panicked, Barton might have gotten away with it. That gun wasn't registered. He could have said it was Shay's and Shay was showing it to him when it went off and the shooting was an accident. There weren't any powder burns on Shay like there would have been if Barton stuck the gun in his chest and pulled the trigger. With the right jury, he could have walked."

"But then Lottie showed up."

Kearny nodded. "Yeah, she complicated things for Barton. I get killing her, but I don't get stealing the song."

"More panic. Danny didn't just kill Eddie, he killed his future. He needed something quick to keep moving with Sunsong and he knew he couldn't do it on his own. He saw that song as his salvation. Maybe he figured Eddie owed it to him for quitting. Maybe there's more to it, but I'm no shrink."

"And what about you? What next?"

"My life won't change much, I suppose. I expect I'll be playing one-nighters 'til I fall off the stool. On another subject, I brought you something."

I pulled a flat, thin box from the bag I was carrying and handed it to Kearny.

"What's this?"

"A little get well present."

He opened the box. In it was a red and blue striped tie. It was a clip-on. "I figured it would be a while before you could use both hands to tie one."

Someone rapped on the doorjamb. "Hey, partner!" A stocky black man in sweats who looked as if he had muscles in his feces walked in carrying a small paper bag. He dumped a half-dozen cans of Skoal on Kearny's nightstand. "In case you run low."

"How long you think I'm gonna be in here?"

"Not long enough for me to clean up the goddamned mess you left at the office. That's what you get for chasin' dangerous felons without your highly capable partner." He turned to me. "You Sam Dunne?" I nodded and he held out a hand for me to shake. "Devon Wilson." He pronounced it "Dee-Von," emphasis on the Dee. His handshake was controlled but it let me know who spent more time in the gym. Devon grinned. "I hear you saved this clown's life. I don't know whether to thank you or shoot you, he's such a pain in my balls."

Kearny piped up, "Don't shoot him 'til I'm done with him."

I laughed and said, "I'll leave you two to your reunion."

I was almost out the door when Kearny said, "Hey, Sam."

I looked back. He gave me the three count and said, "I was wrong about you. I guess you could kill somebody."

"And Wendy was right about you. You're a damned good cop."

41

The rest you probably know. Kearny moved up a step to Chief of Detectives. Wendy's book *Dead Man's Melody* is on the *New York Times* Top Ten, and she's making the rounds of the talk shows. I saw her on *Jumpstart* a few weeks ago. I don't think they'll invite her back after the hash she made of Donna Fields. Blue Smoke will be out of jail soon. Once the murder rap went away his lawyers argued down the charges from dealing to simple possession and a couple of traffic violations once a few of the right people heard from Tiny. Cotton is still playing at the Regent; a few things in life stay the same.

In the meantime, my Sunsong LP *Requiem*, with my own tribute to Eddie and a song for Lottie, hit number twenty-four for two weeks. No illusions: I admit a lot of the sales were boosted by my temporary notoriety, but at least I won't be eating dog food in my old age. Jenny moved in with me last month, and there's not enough room in the apartment for her stuff and mine. I guess it's time for a bigger space. Maybe once in a while Indian Summer does last. "The best is yet to be."

Amen.

ABOUT OUR CREATORS

AUTHOR -

FRED ADAMS Jr. - is a western Pennsylvania native who has enjoyed a lifelong love affair with horror, fantasy, and science fiction literature and films. He holds a Ph.D. in American Literature from Duquesne University and recently retired from teaching writing and literature in the English Department of Penn State University.

Fred is also a lifetime guitarist who still performs solo and with bands in the western Pennsylvania area. His new non-fiction book on the music life, *Twenty Frets, no Nets: Advice for the Solo Guitarist* is available from Amazon.com and Amazon Kindle. Check out his website: http://drphreddee.com

He has published over 50 short stories in amateur, and professional magazines and anthologies as well as hundreds of news features as a staff writer and sportswriter for the now *Pittsburgh Tribune-Review.* In the 1970s Fred published the fanzine *Spoor* and its companion *The Spoor Anthology.* Since 2014 Airship 27 has published two novels in his Hitwolf series, two in his Six-Gun Terror series, and *C. O. Jones: Mobsters and Monsters,* plus including his stories and novellas in their anthologies, including *Secret Agent X vol. 5,* and *All-American Sports Stories vol. 1.* His second C. O. Jones novel, *Skinners* and a second Sam Dunne Novel, *Blood is the new Black,* are forthcoming from Airship 27 in the near future.

● ● ●

INTERIOR ILLUSTRATIONS –

RICHARD JUN - Rich Jun is an aspiring comic book illustrator and a professional doctor of optometry. He spent most of his formative years pouring over comic books. He carefully and meticulously copied the likes of Art Adams, John Buscema, John Byrne and Jim Lee. He majored in drawing and painting at Loyola University in Chicago and was awarded scholarships to attend summer classes at the Art Institute of Chicago. After graduation, Rich worked odd jobs but struggled to crack into the art world.

Keen at making his own way in the world independent from his parents, he went to graduate school to become an eye doctor. He ventured off to New York City for graduate school and loved every minute of it. Rich has spent the last ten years treating patients from eye diseases and preventing blindness. All the while, he continued his affair with comic books and action figures.

Rich lives in Madison Wisconsin with his lovely girlfriend and two rescued pit bulls. One day while perusing the mail, they came across a comic book art class. She encouraged him to jump in and everything changed. Rich met his instructor, Jeff Butler, and continued to study with him for two years. Under Jeff's tutelage, his aspirations have reignited.

Rich is grateful and thrilled to work under the incredible Airship 27 with Ron Fortier and Rob Davis.

• • •

COVER ARTIST –

ROB DAVIS - began his professional art career doing illustrations for role-playing games in the late 1980's. Not long after he began lettering and inking, then penciling comics for a number of small black and white comics publishers- most notably for Eternity Comics, which eventually became Malibu Comics in the 1990's, on their book SCIMIDAR with writer R.A. Jones. Branching out to other black and white publishers and eventually working at both DC and Marvel Rob worked on likeness intensive comics like TV adaptations of QUANTUM LEAP and STAR TREK's many incarnations mostly on the DEEP SPACE NINE comics for Malibu. At Marvel he worked on the Saturday morning cartoon adaptation PIRATES OF DARK WATER. After the comics industry implosion in the late 1990's Rob picked up work on video games, advertising illustration and T-shirt design as well as some small press comics like ROBYN OF SHERWOOD for Caliber. Rob continues to do the odd self-published comic book as well as publisher and designer for his small-press production REDBUD STUDIO COMICS. Rob is Art Director, Designer and Illustrator for the New Pulp production outfit AIRSHIP 27 partnered with writer/editor Ron Fortier. Rob is the recipient of the PULP FACTORY AWARD for "Best Interior Illustrations" in 2010 for his work on SHERLOCK HOLMES: CONSULTING DETECTIVE and has been nominated for the same award every year since. He works and lives in central Missouri with his wife and two children.